The Monster of Matlock

Author's original edited version 1.1

eBook ISBN 978-0-9872720-9-6

Paperback ISBN 978-0-6480789-7-5

Aenghus Chisholme

Connect with Aenghus Chisholme: www.aenghuschisholme.com

Cover by Susan Krupp

Also, by Aenghus Chisholme

Merlin the Sorcerer AD491

Guinevere the Queen AD494

Sir Gawain and the Green Knight AD499

Arthur the King AD517

Murder on the Mary Celeste

Jack the Ripper: The Murder of Madam Athalia

The Best Things in Life Begin with the Letter B

This book is dedicated to those that face a challenge bravely

Table of Contents

Chapter 1: Outside of Matlock Village, Derbyshire England 1893

It was a moonless night. A lone walker wished for the comfort of a fire. It was cold; the 18th of January. He shouldn't have been out walking when he did. The days are so short at this time of year, and he knew it. Knew better than to hike into the hills of Matlock too late into the afternoon. But even with all of this common sense he had managed to lose track of time and get himself into a position where he could not possibly get back to his cottage before facing complete darkness.

A branch hit his face as he tenderly moved forward. He mumbled with indignation. Slightly flustered, he pushed it away from his face and paused to look around him. He was still on the regular walking path that he and so many others had worn-in over the years. If he kept on it, he would reach the 'Cricketer's Bat', his favourite pub. Then he could refresh himself before continuing to his home.

The thought warmed him despite the cold wind blowing. He was about to continue when a sound pervaded his consciousness. It was something that he had never heard before. The wind blowing in his ears prevented him from immediately discerning which direction it was coming from. It sounded like a simultaneous bubbling and slithering noise. It was quite perplexing.

He was still pondering the noise, unknowingly erroneously looking ahead to see if he could find its source when there was another strange occurrence. He could see the surrounding trees and pathway much more clearly now. It was being lit in the most bizarre green colour. At first, he could not tell from where the light source was emanating. But a shadow on the ground in front of him startled the man. He jumped a little as did the shadow. It was his. In a flash of realisation, he knew that the green light and peculiar noise were coming from behind him.

He spun around; a hideous sight greeted him. A glowing-green shapeless blob of quivering jelly was moving toward him. It was about his height and rough dimensions but was completely devoid of features. Where there should have been a face was simply a glowing and pulsating globule.

Fear gripped the man so tightly that he stopped breathing. He couldn't even muster the ability to scream. The thing shot out a tentacle towards him narrowly missing him and landing somewhere to his side. Blind panic replaced his breathless fear and the man turned and ran forward as fast as his legs would carry him. He was completely unaware of his limbs propelling him forward at a speed that he had probably never achieved at any time previously in his life.

Adrenaline coursed through his veins so fully that such things as caution and fatigue were completely eliminated. He ran for his life.

***

The cold evening was not evident in the somewhat remote Cricketer's Bat pub. A huge inglenook fireplace with a well stoked fire heated the pub throughout. It was not particularly crowded. Nor was it bereft of patrons. There were a number of the locals enjoying the warmth of the inn and the company of each other.

Everyone had a drink of some kind or the other. There were two men playing a game of darts in the far corner with some other of the patrons acting as their audience. Others sat in small groups or in couples chatting. The sound of laughter interspersed with the clinking of glasses completed the friendly ambience of the inn.

The front door to the pub was suddenly cast open with such ferocity that it slammed into the beamed wall where it came to a noisy halt. Mister Albert Brawnly almost toppled into the pub along with the door. Everyone stopped what they were doing and looked up at him.

He was clearly very distressed, breathing hard with a look of fright on his weathered face.

It didn't take long for the cold outside to make its presence felt too.

"It nearly got me!" shouted Albert looking around at the faces of everyone staring at him. Then as if he suddenly remembered something, Albert twirled around to look outside.

"What in God's name are you doing Albert" shouted the publican. A man of stout height and broad width. He started walking out from behind the bar toward the front door as he spoke.

"Close the door. You're letting all of the heat out!" he admonished Albert.

But Albert did not need cajoling. He reached for the heavy door and slammed it shut. Taking particular effort to push the latch downwards, ensuring that it was latched. Albert backed his bodyweight up to the door as if bracing it from an assault from outside.

"Horrible, it were..,horrible!" Albert's face contorted as he pictured the creature that had so terrified him.

"What was horrible?" demanded the publican quite annoyed at the behaviour of one of his regular clients.

"Something…something…something out there. It were behind me. Glowing green; and with tentacles like a giant squid from the deep. The kind that drags sailors to their deaths" Albert was verging on being hysterical.

The reference to a squid so far inland was perplexing enough to all present, but the overall summation of what had so upset Albert was simply unbelievable. The publican put into words what everybody was already thinking.

"You're drunk!" he said in a heavily-accusatory tone.

"No. No I'm not. But that's the thing. I need a drink. Oh, for pity's sake get me a drink to settle my nerves." Albert's plea had such a note of compassion to it, that the publican threw his arms into the air in a motion of surrender.

"Alright Albert. I'll get you your usual" he said.

“No, not a lager something stronger. Look at me I’m shaking through and through” Again the sincerity in Albert’s voice garnered acquiescence from the publican.

“Fine. One whisky coming up” he said heading back to his usual position behind the bar so that he could fulfil the order.

“You say a giant squid has frightened you?” It was the mayor talking now. Some people laughed thinking that he was making fun of Albert. But Thaddeus Tremorlund was not joking at all. He was genuinely concerned for what had caused Albert Brawnly’s uncharacteristic outburst.

Albert was collecting his thoughts now. The publican was walking toward him with the whisky in hand. Albert grabbed the glass and downed the lot in one gulp.

“Steady on Albert” cautioned the publican.

“Another, please Iain; I need it!” pleaded Albert.

In another show of surrender, Iain the publican recovered the glass from Albert and proceeded back to his bar so that he could pour him another one.

“Come over here Albert” invited the mayor “Sit down with me and tell me all about it” Albert moved over to where Thaddeus was sitting. The mayor’s companion pulled out a chair so that Albert could join them.

“You don’t mind do you Michael?” inquired Thaddeus of his friend. Mister Michael Thomas Morrell was a stately and kindly old man in his seventies. He smiled as he responded.

“Not at all Thaddeus. Yes, please Albert. Tell us all about this squid” invited Mister Morrell.

"It weren't a squid. Just had a tentacle like a squid. It were, green and glowing and…" He said as he took his seat; still the centre of attention for everyone in the pub. Albert stopped speaking for a moment, trying to gather his thoughts some more. It gave the mayor a chance to ask questions.

"Where did you see this..thing? If it wasn't a squid, exactly what was it?"

Thaddeus looked at Albert evenly, trying to judge the state of mind of the man. Iain arrived with the second whisky and handed it to the eagerly awaiting recipient.

Albert drank it down. A little slower than the first one, but still unconscionably quick for the spirit. Whisky, after all, was supposed to be savoured. Iain rolled his eyes at the uncouthness of the display. He once again recovered the glass and before Albert could ask for another he pointed a thick finger right into his face and warned him.

"I'll get you your usual lager this time Albert. You've had enough whisky to settle the nerves of a raging bull". The reference brought laughter from the other patrons.

Albert looked firstly at Iain and then at the mayor and then at Michael Morrell. He realised now that he must have been presenting quite a spectacle. But it was understandable under the circumstances. He nodded to Iain in agreement.

Albert then attempted to put into words a more cohesive account of what he had encountered. Everyone was paying close attention.

"I was out walking; you know, like I do. But I wandered too far from home given the time of year and how quick it gets dark, you know. It were dark and I was heading here, so that I could fortify myself for the onward journey home. I heard a strange sound, saw a strange light. I realised that it were coming from behind me. I turned to see a green mound of moving….puss", It was all he could think of to describe the shapeless thing.

"A horrible creature it were chasing me. It had a tentacle that reached out to grab me; but I ran. Ran like the wind for fear of my life."

"Did it chase you?" asked Thaddeus.

"God only knows. I didn't look back to see" replied Albert.

"Well, let's see if it did in fact pursue you here?" stated the mayor in his typical officious tone. He stood up and made to go to the door. Albert was blinded by panic once more and he grabbed the mayor's arm.

"Don't open the door, it may be there!" he yelled. But Thaddeus Tremorlund would not be dissuaded from his investigation. He pulled Arthur's hand from his forearm and marched brazenly toward the door. There was a small murmur from those present of either discontent with the proposed action, or support, it was hard to tell. He stopped and put his hand on the latch.

"Don't!" pleaded Albert.

Silence and anticipation could be felt in equal amounts filling the pub as surely as the fire filled the room with warmth. The mayor paused either for dramatic effect or perhaps because he was reconsidering his actions. Then he pulled up the latch and flung the door open.

Some people recoiled in a reflex motion, others leant forward in expectation of seeing the glowing green creature with tentacles described by Albert. There was nothing but the darkness of the rolling hillside, incomprehensible in the night, and the cold wind once more robbing the pub of its cosiness.

Satisfied that there was no waiting monster. Thaddeus closed and relatched the wooden door. He turned to Albert with a look of scorn on his face.

"Is your *creature* not up for a pint Albert?"

The mayor's sarcastic jibe was met with a round of laughter from everyone in the room except Albert.

"I know what I saw" insisted Albert. By this time Ian the publican had pulled a good pint of lager and delivered it to the table. Albert reached for the glass handle and took a swig.

Other patrons now seemingly bored with the story began to converse with their groups again. As the pub returned to the former social atmosphere that Albert had interrupted so abruptly, the mayor contemplated his next move. He returned to the table.

"How is Martha, Michael. Well I trust?" Thaddeus was inquiring about Michael Morell's good wife.

"Yes, indeed thank you Thaddeus. Very well; and no-doubt waiting for me to arrive so that we may have our supper. So, it if all the same to you, and providing there is not a glowing green squid out there waiting for me. I'll bid you a good night." Michael Morell stood up preparing to leave.

"Please pass on my best regards" asked the mayor.

"I shall Thaddeus. Good night Albert"

"I wouldn't be going out there if I were you" pleaded Albert. But Michael would hear none of it. He had already convinced himself that the man was suffering a delusion of some description. Imagine, a squid in the middle of the Derbyshire countryside? Poppycock. How exactly would it have come to Matlock? By swimming up the Derwent river that snakes its way through the town centre? And how would a salt-water beast live in a fresh water river? A myriad of questions all very damning of Albert Brawnly's account of what had purportedly happened to him were in Michael's mind. However, he was far too much of a gentleman to give voice to any of them.

But Michael Morrell's thoughts were now setting upon the walk up the hill and making it home in time to have supper with his wife, Martha.

The pub was basically out on its own on the hillside. It was between Balmoral house, where Michael and Martha resided, and The Rockside hydropathic centre, one of the three largest of the spa resorts in Matlock. There was very little by way of buildings around, save for the occasional small stone cottage built in the style so popular in this part of Derbyshire.

The walk in the dark was not without its hazards. The steep rolling hills that Matlock and the surrounding townships were built upon held traps for the unwary. Steep ravines close to the walking paths and others not so steep but easily able to inflict much harm should he fall into one of them. These were of more concern to Michael than a fictitious creature roaming the pathway home.

Being a sensible man, he had prepared for the journey and took out his portable brass oil lamp. It would be recognised by anyone as the type that the railway workers used. Small, efficient and able to light the pathway before him with enough illumination to ensure his safe passage.

"Try to get some rest Albert" coaxed Michael. "You look tired." Michael put enough coins on the table to cover the cost of his drink with the mayor. With his verbal farewells complete Michael nodded his silent farewell to the publican and to the others that he made eye contact with as he strode brazenly out of the inn.

Albert watched Michael leave with a rising feeling of trepidation. As if able to read the man's feelings Thaddeus offered Albert his drink. He pushed the small tumbler of whisky toward Albert.

"I think that you need this more than I" he said.

Albert took a swig of the offered spirit and washed it down with a mouthful of his lager.

“I’ll get myself another one” said Thaddeus and strolled over to the bar to do so.

When he returned Albert was looking around the pub as if seeking unspoken support from anyone that they believed what he had told all of them.

“Of course, it would be terrible” said Thaddeus.

Albert completely misunderstood the context of the sentence and nodded his head.

“It were terrible; horrible thing it were” he reiterated.

Thaddeus gave him an annoyed look and corrected Albert’s understanding of his point.

“I meant that it would be terrible for Matlock if we were to be branded as having a local monster Albert”.

At first Albert did not understand what the mayor meant.

“Eh?” Albert queried.

The mayor expanded upon his thinking.

“Imagine what it would do for our tourist population Albert? Matlock survives by the thousands of tourists that travel here every year to take in the healing mineral waters at all the local spa establishments. Should the word get out that we have a monster I can see one of two things happening. And they are both terrible” he said hoping that the point was getting through to Albert.

A dumbfounded shake of his head alerted Thaddeus that he would need to continue to make the point in more detail.

“Either our life’s-blood, cash-bearing tourists, would stay away in droves, causing hereto unheard-of economic woes for our town, or we would be overrun with monster-hunters. And they aren't the kind that spend weeks at a spa or spending their much-needed money in our town shops. We would be the laughing stock of the country. It would be an absolutely awful outcome Albert. Do you see now?"

The mayor's tone had such conviction in it that, even though Albert did not completely comprehend the problem, he nodded in agreement.

"I knew that you would see it my way" smiled Thaddeus. "Finish your drinks, and you may have mine as well. I am sure that your nerves need a little more quelling. Am I correct?" The mayor put on his best statesman-like smile. And it won-over Albert in a heartbeat.

Albert proceeded to finish off the whisky that Thaddeus had given him and reach for the one that had replaced it. Whisky with a lager chaser. It was exactly what Albert needed right now.

***

By the time that the pub crowd had thinned out Albert was very drunk indeed. Helped surreptitiously by the mayor who insisted on plying him with drinks that he told Iain the publican was in fact for himself. But Mayor Tremorlund was acting out of self-interest. That is, his interest in not seeing this ridiculous story spreading further than it had already gone.

One of the other patrons approached.

"Looks like you may need help getting home Albert"

Both Albert and Thaddeus looked up. It was Keith Smedley, the current manager of Smedley's Hydropathic Establishment. Keith Smedley was in no way related to John Smedley the original founder who had died about five years ago. It was just happenstance that they both shared the same surname.

Albert objected.

"I am fine thank you very much" he said with unusual pauses between each slurred word.

"Of course, you are" patronised Keith Smedley. However, the tone and obvious sarcastic reference were completely lost on Albert in his inebriated state.

"I'll see to our highly-imaginative friend" said the mayor.

Keith smiled and nodded and went back to the table that he had been sitting at with two others. Thaddeus leant forward.

"I think that the best course of action is to put all of this behind you Albert. A good night's sleep is what you need."

It sounded perfectly reasonable to Albert in his current condition. In fact, it sounded exactly what he suddenly felt like doing. Tiredness was overwhelming him. The alcohol had dulled the fear of the glowing creature to such a point that he was now even doubting himself that he saw it in the first place.

"I'm going home" he said, slowly and deliberately announcing each word as carefully as he was currently capable of.

“Let me see you to the door; and take my lamp to light your way” offered Thaddeus in a hushed voice, ensuring that nobody else would hear him.

To the rest of the crowd it looked for all intents and purposes that they were leaving together. Thaddeus settled the bill for both himself and Albert, put on his coat and handed the lamp to Albert who was visibly swaying on his feet. The mayor lit it with a match and they both waved goodbye to all and strode out of the door, closing it behind them. It would be the last time that any of them saw Albert Brawnly alive.

Outside, the mayor pointed Albert in the direction of his home and set him in motion. Unable to resist or even care what was happening to him at this stage, Albert complied by stumbling forward, the lamp amply lighting his way.

The mayor waited for a good two minutes and then re-entered the pub. People looked up in confusion as he walked in.

“Wouldn’t accept my company to see him safely home. Looks like the squid-creature is a distant memory to Albert now.”

“Found some Dutch courage by the look of it” said someone. Thaddeus didn’t see who it was, but did acknowledge the comment.

“I’m sure he will be fine when he’s slept it off.” Thaddeus walked over to the fire to warm his hands. He stood there for a few minutes glancing sideways at the patrons. He was furtively keeping a close eye on all of them.

Another darts game was beginning in the far corner of the pub. It was exactly the distraction that the mayor needed. As people made their way over to watch the game he backed away slowly, making his way to the back of the bar and when he was sure that nobody was looking, snuck out via the scullery and the pub's back door.

As he left he noticed that he could not see Keith Smedley anywhere. He wondered what had become of the man. He could not recollect seeing him leave the inn; nobody had. But for now, he was content with slipping away unobserved.

Chapter 2: Later That Night

Michael Morrell had indeed made it home in plenty of time to have supper with his wife Martha. They enjoyed a lovely dinner of roast pork and boiled vegetables that was prepared by Missus Lister, the housekeeper that they employed. A necessary expense given the size of Balmoral House where they resided. Martha was simply not able to upkeep the rather stately manor home all by herself. Missus Lister had served up the dinner and left them to enjoy it in peace.

Michael had much interesting gossip to impart to Martha from his drink with Mayor Thaddeus Tremorlund. However, that paled by comparison to the story that he regaled Martha with, about poor old Albert Brawnly bursting into the pub spouting a tale about a green monster that had so terrified him.

"Good heavens; what an imagination!" Martha had exclaimed. Much like her husband she had dismissed the idea out of hand completely. Monsters simply do not exist in the physical world. She above most people knew that. But in the ethereal world of those that had passed on; that was another matter entirely.

There was no thought that Albert Brawnly had encountered a ghost of any description. He would have needed to be a *sensitive* like Martha to be capable of conjuring up an apparition. Martha was by no means a Psychic, like her deceased sister Alice Athalia, but was still very much able to sense when a ghostly-presence was near. She had sensed no such thing during the evening. And so sure was she of her abilities in this area, that it completely precluded the idea that it may have been an other-worldly appearance.

They continued to chat for the remainder of the evening after finishing dinner and packing up the dishes in the kitchen ready for Missus Lister to take care of tomorrow. They sat by the fire with Michael reading the daily paper and occasionally passing comment or sharing a story of interest with Martha. Martha worked diligently on her knitting. This particular item was a shawl for one of their nieces that lived in London. Martha's abilities in knitting were somewhat formidable as well. The completed product would be so professionally constructed that it would be indistinguishable from a high-street offering.

Such was the life of this retired couple. Michael had made his fortune in the manufacturing of sewing needles. The money that he made from the sale of the company that he built from nothing to a major supplier to the entire country, had funded the purchase of their home here in Matlock.

The original stone cottage had been purchased whilst they still lived in London. The cottage in Matlock had been totally refurbished and expanded until it became the stately manor house that they now lived in together. Retirement suited them both. Michael was now seventy-eight years of age and Martha seventy-four. Matlock was a sleepy little town in the heart of

Derbyshire, and it attracted them both as an escape from the frenetic life in London that they had lived.

Eventually though, as the evening wore on, they both tired and decided to retire for the night.

***

It was about three o'clock in the morning when Martha had a disturbing dream. She was walking alone in the woods on the slopes of Matlock. Martha recognised the place. It was quite a well-trodden pathway. The one that led to Cavendish Road. This section of it was heavily forested though. The only other point of interest would be the Cricketer's Bat Inn further up the trail.

It was neither dark nor light. It was an indeterminable time of day, or night. First light of morning, or dusk in the evening would have best described it, but even they would fall short in this instance. Martha walked along the pathway admiring the stillness of the surrounds. It was so peaceful here. Unusually peaceful. No birds, no sound of wind in the trees, nothing.

It became harder to move. Something prevented Martha from being able to lift her legs. They felt weighed-down with lead. The feeling was alarming. Martha looked about her. Suddenly there was somebody further up the trail. A young girl. Martha couldn't quite see her properly. But no matter, the young lass was walking toward her.

“Can you please help me?” called out Martha to the youngster.

The girl continued to walk toward Martha at the same pace as if oblivious to the plea. Martha thought to call out again but instead waited for the girl to approach. As she did so Martha recognised her, but for the life of her, couldn’t remember where from.

The blonde-haired girl was fresh faced, about the age of seventeen. She was dressed in a blue flowing dress that looked incredibly soft, as if it were made from the finest silk. She stopped about ten-feet away from Martha and smiled at her.

Martha smiled back; there was something so very familiar about this girl, if only she could put her finger on it. While she was still wondering, the face of the girl began to age. Years past by in a matter of seconds. The once young girl was easily now in her twenties, thirties, fourties, fifties and then instantly Martha recognised her.

“Alice! I didn’t recognise you my dear, you were so young”

Before Martha now stood Alice Athalia, Martha’s deceased sister. Martha realised immediately that she was having a vision within a dream. And what a lovely dream to see her sister once more. The years continued to transform Alice until she looked exactly as Martha remembered the last time that she had seen her alive. Now in her eighties, Alice was a picture of beautifully-matured womanhood.

“Alice my dear, how are you? What wisdom from the after-life do you have for me?”

Martha was genuinely elated to be conversing with her sister once more. Alice had died just under five years ago, in London. But Martha wasn’t interested in that now. She had her sister to speak with from the great beyond. And she was going to avail herself of the incredible opportunity that it afforded.

But it was not to be; Alice spoke, but Martha could not hear the words coming from her sister’s mouth.

“I cannot hear you Alice” said Martha somewhat alarmed now.

For her part Alice was pointing to something behind Martha. Martha looked around as much as she could with her legs now seemingly solidified into the ground. There was nothing.

“I don’t understand Alice, there is nothing there? What are you trying to tell me?”

Martha pleaded with Alice to give her answers. None came. Instead Alice was now gestures with her hands. It was enormously frustrating.

“Come over here Alice, take my hands” offered Martha. Hopefully they could share a psychic connection. That would alleviate the need to speak words in order to communicate. But Alice was shaking her head. She pointed to her legs. They had sunk into the ground up to her ankles. Martha was shocked. She looked down at her own legs and found that they had suffered a similar fate.

“What does it mean?” implored Martha of her sister.

Alice began to gesture with her hands once more. Martha was distraught at their shared situation but did her best to try and interpret what Alice was trying to convey. Martha concentrated on the mime that unfurled before her. Alice seemed to be pointing at the two of them and then shaking her head furiously. Martha thought briefly and then offered her initial interpretation.

“Women, that is what we are. But you are pointing at us and shaking your head. Are you saying that what you need to tell me is about a man?” Martha was clutching at straws really, but willing to try anything to further this exchange between them.

Alice smiled broadly and nodded her head in affirmation. Then she proceeded to point at her buried feet and Martha’s too and made gestures as if they should be moving instead of frozen in place.

“A man walking?” offered Martha. Alice nodded again. The next action that Alice made was to point at the trail behind Martha, between them and onwards up the rather steep incline.

“A man walking on this trail?” Martha was surer of her interpretation this time and rightly so. Alice confirmed that she was correct. But Alice’s next indication was of horror. She twisted her face and looked terrified, screaming a cry that could not be heard.

"A man walking on this trail sees something horrible?" Martha was rewarded with a nod once more. It did not take long for Martha to put the pieces together.

"Alice are you trying to tell me something about the fright that Albert Brawnly suffered this evening?" Once more Martha's interpretation of the message was perfect.

"Alice, are you trying to tell me that the creature that Albert Brawnly saw was from the afterlife?"

No; Alice was shaking her head.

"Are you saying that it was real?"

Yes, Alice was nodding her head and mouthing the word clearly, even though there was frustratingly still no sound heard.

"Albert did not imagine this creature. It is real and it is a threat to us and to our village?"

Again, the word yes was mouthed and indicated by Alice. Martha was worried. She needed to know much more.

"That is dreadful news Alice. What is this creature? Where does it come from? What does it want? Does it wish us harm……?."

Martha realised that she was now alone. Alice had disappeared. The surroundings were looking darker now. Martha felt her legs released from their earthly trap. She was floating upwards into the sky. The peace of sleep enfolded her once more and Martha continued to sleep for the remainder of the night.

Chapter 3: The Following Day

Another walker along the steep inclines and declines of the pathways criss-crossing the hills of Matlock had no idea of what he was about to encounter. But he was not alone. Cavalier, his Border Collie was with him. The dog, full of energy was running ahead of the man. This particular section of the pathway had a cliff face rising to the left and a sloping decline to the right.

The pathway was etched into the flattest part of the area. He was approaching a part of it with quite tall grass near the bottom of the cliff above. Cavalier jumped into the grassy area disappearing temporarily from view. The hound began to bark. It must have found a fox hole or something thought the man. Cavalier loved to hunt foxes. It was one of his favourite things to do.

The man called out to the animal.

“What have you found there boy? Another fox-hole I’ll bet. Let’s take a look”

The man could hear the dog panting and barking. He approached the grass and parted the area that he had seen his dog jump into. The body of a man lay there with the dog looking down at him, licking the man’s face. From the angle of the limbs and the head to the neck it was immediately clear that the man was deceased.

"Come away!" he commanded the dog, who obediently obeyed and took his place at the heel of the man.

"Oh my god, that poor fellow" said the man.

He looked up to the cliff-top above him. That was the pathway that led to the Cricketer's Bat Inn. There was one section that was particularly perilous. And some poor sole had come asunder because of it. He was still wondering at the circumstances that had seen the unfortunate fellow loose his way from the pathway above and fall down the cliff to his death here below, when he noticed something. He knew the face of the man.

"Albert Brawnly" he said aloud. "Bless my soul; and may God rest yours in peace"

The man knew Albert Brawnly enough to wish him a good morning, day or evening. They were acquaintances, not friends. Nevertheless, he was very distraught at seeing the man here now dead before him.

"Poor Albert" said the man. Cavalier responded with a woof. The man looked down at the dog.

"We had better get the authorities eh boy?"

***

Word had spread throughout Matlock of the demise of Albert Brawnly. By the time his body was transported to the mortuary in the basement of the local hospital just about everybody had heard the sad news.

Chief of Police in the area, Captain Perry Wiksworth had ordered his constables to investigate the scene for any sign of possible wrong-doing. Doctor William Moxton had been called in by the police to examine the body for the same reason. He was looking over Albert Brawnley's now naked body on a table in the poorly lit mortuary of the small Matlock Hospital. Captain Wiksworth was with him.

"Nothing untoward that I can see from an initial examination Captain. I can tell from the smell around the mouth that he would have been somewhat intoxicated with a mixture of lager and whisky. Death by way of a broken neck and trauma to the head, no-doubt sustained in the fall from the cliff" Doctor Moxton concluded the brief summation of his findings.

Captain Wiksworth nodded.

"That would be consistent with the information that I have gathered so far from the inn keeper, nearest to where the body was found. Apparently, the deceased was in the Cricketer's Bat Pub for quite some time. Ranting about seeing a monster in the woods."

Doctor Moxton, a sensible and well-educated man in his fifties, raised an eyebrow.

"Indeed? Did he say exactly what *kind* of monster?" The note of incredulity was evident in his voice.

"Apparently Mayor Tremorlund allayed his fears regarding the sighting. I will know more when I have spoken to the mayor."

"Will you be requiring a full autopsy? If so may I suggest one of the surgeons from…" Doctor Moxton did not get to complete his recommendation.

"At this stage Doctor, it is looking very much like the deceased was intoxicated and on the pathway, that would return him to his cottage, stumbled off the pathway in the darkness and met with an ignominious end. Nothing more than an unfortunate accident."

It was clear that the Captain did not think that there would be too much to this case.

"Very well then. I will write-up my findings and deliver them to the Police station before noon today" offered the good Doctor.

"I would be very grateful to you Doctor Moxton. Thank you for agreeing to do the examination of the body".

"You are very welcome Captain. Well if there is nothing else? I will be on my way" The doctor moved over to the side table where a washbowl and hot water and soap awaited him. He would meticulously clean his hands after the examination of the corpse.

"Nothing else Doctor Moxton, I will not impose upon anymore of your time. And I must be getting over to the Town Hall to speak with the mayor." He verbalised his plans as he gathered his hat and coat and left the Doctor to complete his washing ritual.

***

The town hall was an imposing two-story rectangular building made of stone. It was distinguished by the set of five oversized arched windows on each side for the upper level. The front had two similar windows on the upper level and a bull-nosed section to the right of the external staircase.

Captain Wiksworth ascended the stairs and opened the outer door. Inside was a foyer that was large enough to accommodate many hats and coats. He found a suitable rack and relieved himself of them. Then entering the inner door, he faced the inner staircase that led upwards to the main hall. But it was the offices down here on the elevated ground floor that he was interested in.

He passed by a number of the office doors until he came across the regalest looking one of them. Mayor Thaddeus Tremorlund was painted in gold-leaf on the centre of the door. Even though it was a heavy wooden door with what looked to be many coats of black lacquer, he could hear voices coming from inside.

He knocked. The voices fell silent. He opened the door. Inside he could see what the villagers all referred to as the two T's. Thaddeus and his wife Tiffany. Other than them, there was no one. If Captain Wiksworth had been able to influence such things as nick-names for people, he would have branded them the four T's. It seemed more appropriate given the couple shared names that were essentially alliteration.

“Am I interrupting something?” inquired Captain Wiksworth. And it did look like he was doing just that. They both had looks of guilt on their faces as if they had been caught doing something that they shouldn’t.

“Not at all Perry, do please come in” Tiffany’s over-zealous happiness irked the Captain somewhat, but he did not let it show. At his stage of life, a dignified sixty he was more than capable of hiding his true feelings.

“I suppose that you’ve heard about Albert Brawnly?” Perry inquired.

“Yes, dreadful shock it was too if you don’t mind my saying” offered Thaddeus.

Captain Wiksworth entered the room and closed the door behind him. Tiffany offered him a seat which he took. She remained standing beside her husband who sat in a large green leather chesterfield chair on the other side of a rather huge desk.

“You understand that I have to investigate this death even though it seems to be an open and shut case” Perry was being very diplomatic now, not wanting to ruffle the Mayor’s feathers.

“Of course, Perry; we understand completely. Don’t we my dear?” said the mayor looking up at his wife for affirmation.

“Oh yes, yes, of course we do.” She said in her typically too-happy to be true tone.

“The publican tells me that you left with the deceased around nine pm?” Perry’s first question sounded innocuous enough.

“Ah, yes, that sounds about right. I wanted to walk Albert home. He had been drinking probably a little too much. But he wouldn’t hear of an escort. Insisted that he walk home alone.” Thaddeus almost blurted out the words. Not in his usual stately manner.

“Did he?” inquired Perry.

“Yes! Yes, He was a head-strong fellow poor old Albert Brawnly”

Mayor Tremorlund sounded more perturbed than politician at this point. His wife chipped in.

“Yes, ask anyone Perry, Albert was never one to be told what to do. Thought that he could look after himself.”

Tiffany had lost her over-joyous tone.

Captain Wiksworth couldn’t quite put his finger on it, but the vilification of Albert Brawnly’s character seemed inappropriate given the circumstances. It was unlike the both of them. But, he thought, it could just be that it was a distressing occurrence in an otherwise sleepy township. Or, it could be guilt at not insisting that he see Albert safely home. He decided to pursue this line of thought.

“If you had insisted on seeing Albert safely home he would still be with us today?”

The question was rhetorical, but Captain Wiksworth expected a response. There was an awkward silence for a few seconds before both Thaddeus and Tiffany began speaking; talking over the top of one another.

"Who's to say…"

"We cannot possible be sure of that…."

Captain Perry Wiksworth was perplexed at the vehemency of the responses. He was expecting something more circumspect from the mayor. Perry regarded them both looking from one to the other unsure of why they were behaving so unusually.

For their part, Thaddeus and Tiffany cast a look to each other. One of alarm. After a short while Perry decided to break the silence.

"I will continue my investigations of course, but to be frank, if nothing else comes to light, I will be forced to conclude death by misadventure."

Both Tremorlunds could be seen to breath a visible sigh of relief. This too puzzled the Captain. He sensed that this occurrence meant more to the mayor and his wife than they were saying, but what? He wasn't aware of any malice that either held for Albert Brawnly.

"There was one other thing. Something about a monster in the woods?" asked Perry.

"Ravings of a drunken man. I think that Albert must have had a few before coming to the pub. Silly nonsense really. Nothing to it, I am certain of that." Thaddeus had his best mayoral voice working now. It had the hallmarks of a political promise to the masses.

"I'm sure that you are right" offered the Captain.

"Of course, he is!" Tiffany had returned to her irritating gleeful tenor.

The Captain made his goodbyes and excused himself from the mayor's office, insisting that he see himself out. As he collected is hat and coat in the foyer he decided to speak to everyone in the pub that could be identified. There was more to this occurrence that met the eye. And he was determined to get to the bottom of it.

Chapter 4: The Funeral Service

There was a very large turn-out for the funeral service of Albert Brawnly. It was held in the largest of the churches in the town on the Sunday afternoon of the same week in which he had died. Captain Perry Wiksworth had released the body without requiring a full autopsy. As for the number of grievers; perhaps Albert was more popular than anyone had thought before, or perhaps it was the manner of his death that had solicited such sympathy from his fellow townsfolk. At any rate, the service was dignified and the funeral procession from the church to the burial plot located at the rear, was replete with well-dressed and stoic individuals.

Albert was not married and had no other family in the area. So, there was only his friends and neighbours to speak for him in the service. They were the ones asked to throw the first handfuls of soil on the coffin after it was lowered into the ground.

With the final words from the presiding vicar, the crowd was now free to ruminate over the incident. They broke into small crowds and were chatting. But after a while it became obvious that one of the groups was swelling. Something interesting must have been being said there. Bit by bit the smaller groups melted into the largest to hear what was going on.

Martha and Michael Morrell seemed to be at the centre of this group. A latecomer, a stout lady with an oversized hat queried the Morrells to repeat what had been said. Marth raised a hand in acknowledgement and nodded her head.

"My friend's you all know me and know of my dearly departed Sister, Madam Alice Athalia, Psychic and adviser to the heads of Europe. Although I may not have shared my sister's amazing abilities, because we came from the same womb, I am able to see around a few corners."

This garnered a round of agreement from the crowd. Martha continued.

"I had a vision of my sister on the night that Albert Brawnly died. She conveyed to me that the monster that Albert had seen that evening, before taking refuge in the Cricketer's Bat, was in fact real. And it is a danger to us all."

This was shocking news to the crowd. They were clearly agitated Martha faced a volley of questions from the people.

"What is this monster?"

"What does it want?"

"Does it intend to eat us?"

"Did it throw Albert from the cliff?"

"Why hasn't anyone seen it before or since?"

Martha pleaded for silence.

"I don't have the answers to these questions. The ethereal plain is sometimes difficult to gain absolute answers from. In this instance Alice couldn't speak. Or rather, she could speak but I could not hear. We were left communicating with hand gestures and mime. But believe me, if my sister is sending us a warning from the other side, we should all heed it."

Such was the sincerity in Martha's voice that it sent a shiver through everyone there. Listening with increasing alarm was Mayor Thaddeus Tremorlund and his wife. He needed to take matters into his own hands if he was to rescue the situation.

"My friends!" he said bidding for their attention. People obligingly turned to him.

"Let us not be hasty in interpreting this message from beyond the grave. By your own admission Martha, you could not hear what Alice was saying to you. And surely this could have just been a dream and not a deliberate message from the other side? Is it not possible that you have mistaken the dream for a message, or even indeed misinterpreted Alice's meaning, if it was a vision?"

Thaddeus gave Martha his best cautionary look. She responded with a dismissive wave of her hand.

"You may doubt all you want Thaddeus, but I know that Alice is trying to warn us about a danger here in Matlock. We haven't heard the last of this."

Once more the mayor wanted to discredit the assertion.

"Well I for one won't be seduced by tales from the ethereal plain, not least of all in the presence of the house of God."

Thaddeus had made a damaging blow. Technically as good Church of England worshipers, they were not allowed to believe in such things. Even though many of them did. Unless it was a direct message from one of his Angels, then it most certainly did not have the blessing of God above, and could not be relied upon in any way.

He looked around the crowd. He had struck a chord with many of them. Relief swelled up inside of him. Martha gave the mayor a look of annoyance and rolled her eyes. There was nothing more to be said. People would either believe or not; it was as simple as that.

***

The prominent figures of the town had been gathered together by Keith Smedley. They had convened in the evening of the next day at Smedley's hydropathic establishment. A grandiose building of intricately carved stone and roof-top wall ornamentation like the battlements of a castle. At the centre of it was as high tower reaching a majestic seven floors in height, topped with ornamental wrought iron in the outlined shape of a dome and then that too was topped with a wrought iron spire reaching to the sky.

The invitees were mostly the owners of the local and surrounding areas spa establishments. From the most recently opened to the oldest institutions; they were all there. Maximillian Daleford from Daleford hydro. Missus Helena Wildgoose from the Oldham hydro spa. Carl Bell owner of the Belle Vue hydro. Jeremy Manchester of the Manchester House hydro. Mister William Atkins from the Rockside Hydropathic Establishment. George and Charlene Davies from the Tor House hydro centre. Aiden Wellfield from the Wellfield House hydro spa. Stephane Elmtree the owner of Elmtree hydro and Missus Mary Whittaker from the Matlock Bath mineral water works. The primary supplier of artesian mineral waters to most of the spas that did not have a bore of their own to tap the aquifer flowing beneath the town.

Most impressively was the presence of mister Job Smith. The town benefactor that was putting into place the impressive Malvern House hydro. Still someway off, and shaping up to be the equal of the Smedley and Rockside hydro buildings. But more importantly, he was the man that had funded the cable tram car that was almost finished. It ran from Matlock Crown Square and up the steep inclination of Bank Road which at its highest point became Rutland Street. There were stops at Smedley's hydro and then further up the top where the tram terminated at the newly built tram depot, people could disembark for the Rockside hydro and when it opened mid-year the Malvern hydro centre. A very wealthy man, he had got the idea on a visit to San Francisco and travelling on the steep-inclination tram cars there. Rounding out the list of guests was of course Mayor Thaddeus Tremorlund.

The gathering was in Keith Smedley's lecture room. This was on the ground level of the sizeable hotel and used for educational purposes. Guests would often listen to lectures from various health experts that would be employed by

Smedley's for the benefit of their paying guests. But this evening it was full of worried people.

They were mulling around in small groups chatting away. Keith Smedley recognised that everyone on the invite list had arrived and called the meeting to order.

"Thank you everybody for making time to meet here on such short notice. I don't think that after the extraordinary events over the past week that I need to explain why we have gathered. It is to ascertain if there is any weight in the story that Martha Morrell has told at the funeral of Albert Brawnly."

This garnered a rush of comments like

"How can we believe such things?"

"The town will be a circus of monster hunters if this gets out"

"What if there is truth to the story? What do we do?"

"No matter how you look at it, this could spell disaster for business here in Matlock"

Feelings were clearly running high. Keith picked up on the last assertion.

"Yes indeed, Mister Bell; what impact on our businesses will it have should such a story get out. And what if as you say Missus Davis, there *is* truth to the story?"

It appeared that Keith was not coming up with any solutions to the dilemma. The Mayor however, decided that it was time for him to intervene.

"My friends. We all have a vested interest in the town of Matlock and the surrounding areas of Matlock Bath and beyond. There will be always be those that believe in such ridiculous things as monsters and we simply cannot stop that. But what we can do is lead by example"

It sounded plausible enough. But was lacking in detail. He was urged by the crowd to elucidate.

"Whenever the subject is brought up by anyone, be sure to be forceful and discredit it immediately. Don't sit on the fence or dilly-dally; show how strong your opinion is that it is all fanciful rhetoric. We are the leaders of this town and people look to us for guidance. If we act as one and push the same message, then people will take heart and fall into line. I am sure of it"

Thaddeus looked around him to see if his speech was having the desired effect. He could see that it was but wanted to reinforce the point.

"And remember my friends that Chief Perry Wiksworth questioned everybody that was present the night of poor old Albert Brawnly's death, myself included and could find absolutely nothing unusual about the entire incident. In effect, we have the support of the Police in our contention that there is nothing unseemly about this unfortunate death other than appalling circumstances."

He certainly did sound assured of his course of action. And he was correct that all of the people present had a monetary investment in the area and either could not or did not want to lose it. Job Smith was the next to talk. He had everyone's undivided attention.

"Thaddeus, you are correct of course. This is a dangerous situation. We know that people can be far too easily swayed by talk of monsters or the supernatural. People tend to believe what they want to believe and not what is true. It is up to us to help the townsfolk see that the truth is, that Albert Brawnly's death was a tragic accident and that there is nothing more sinister to it than that".

Much like the Mayor, Job Smith had an air of assuredness to his words. And the opinion of such a successful and wealthy and philanthropic man, held a good deal of gravitas with these people. There was a round of agreeing words and tones from the men and women.

Keith Smedley took the initiative to ratify the course of action.

"So, it is settled then. We will manage the situation by speaking with one voice, discrediting the very idea of a monster lurking in the woods. All those in favour?"

He received a raucous "here here!" from everyone.

It appeared to everybody that the monster of Matlock was about to be buried in an avalanche of common-sense and scepticism.

***

For a while the conniving plan from the business owners worked. Gossip was interrupted with hearty opinions such as

“No *monster* has ever been caught in England before nor will it be in the future” and

“There simply couldn’t possibly be any substance to the story, nobody else as seen it, where is the proof?” and

“If you want to remain in the dark-ages and believe nonsense like that you would be better of living in the Orkney islands”

Bit by bit, the very forceful opinions began to be repeated around the town. The hydro owner’s sentiments became the viewpoints of others and so it spread like pollen on the wind. A sense of normalcy returned to Matlock. People went about their day-to-day lives once more in contentment. But it wasn’t to last.

Chapter 5: Thursday 16th February 1893

It was a lunar month since the first sighting of the monster. Again, there was no moon in the sky. It was a dark and cold night. There was freshly fallen snow giving the ground, a light covering of white. It was the same pathway where the monster was sighted the first time. This time it was a man of temperance walking it. He had visited an aged friend in a cottage over the hill and was returning to his small home which was quite some way past the Cricketer's Bat pub. He had overstayed his visitation and lost the light. It was just another obstacle to be overcome before he made his way safely home to stoke a warm fire and settle in for the night.

A mist had arisen in the evening making visibility even more difficult. Normally this was the purview of a morning weather phenomenon. But for whatever reason, a mist had descended upon the hills and valleys of Matlock this evening. Along with the snow it gave an atmospheric look to everything. That is, it would have if he could see it properly in the non-existent moonlight.

Christian Mayweather walked along the pathway as best as he could in the poor light. The combination of snow covering the trail and the lack of moonlight made it difficult to navigate. The wind was blowing up the hillside, carrying with it the chill of the forthcoming night. He continued onward moving forward. There was, after all, no need to look behind him.

But something did make him glance backwards. Maybe it was a sound that attracted his attention, maybe it was pure chance. He glanced behind him and saw a sight that made his heart rise into his throat as if to choke him where he stood.

A pulsating mass of glowing green jelly stood there, barely ten feet away, moving inexorably toward him. It was unlike anything that he had ever seen before in his life. There were tendrils emanating from the side of the thing. Lots of them. Too many to count. One of them seemed to swell in size and lurch forward as if to reach out and grab him. He screamed, turned and ran with all of his might. The survival instinct took over and pushed him forward at break-neck speed. But something within Christian Mayweather, a sense of reason, was curious. What was it? He had to know. Was it following? He turned ever so briefly to see if it was following him. It was. But not so fast as he was receding from its reach.

Then disaster struck. He slipped on the snow-touched ground and went tumbled down. Fear gripped his very soul even more tightly than before. He was no longer running from thing behind him, he was at its mercy. With renewed fear, he clambered to his feet and began running again. Again, he glanced behind him. The thing was making the mist around it glow with an eerie light. But it was not running in pursuit of him.

There was a minor sense of relief, but not enough to make him stop running for his life. Exactly how he managed to navigate the difficult path in the circumstances was not even under consideration at this point. He simply did. And he ran and ran.

***

In a scene echoed only a month before, the heavy wooden door of the Cricketer's Bat Inn was thrown open with such a force that everyone in the pub looked up to see what was happening. Christian Mayweather, clearly panicked, slammed the door and ensured that it latched.

Before anybody had a chance to ask him what was wrong he volunteered the information in a loud voice.

"I've seen it. Seen it with my own eyes, as God is my witness. The monster that chased Albert Brawnly! It chased me up the trail. I had to run for my life to escape it!"

At first there was a stunned silence. Christian was clearly distraught and trying desperately to catch his breath. Then a calamity of questions as people rose from their seats and questioned the man as to what he was talking about. The melee was confusing and upsetting simultaneously.

Iain the owner and bar tender took matters into his hands. He shouted above the cacophony.

"Christian Mayweather, is that you? I never thought that I would see you in my humble establishment. Surely you are teetotaller? And yet clearly drunk if you expect us to believe that you have seen a monster!"

Christian was immediately put out at the very thought of touching the devil's drink.

"I've never touched a drop in my entire life. I am not drunk. But I have seen a glowing green monster just as was described by Albert Brawly before his untimely death. It's true. All of it. Green, with tentacles and horrible absolutely horrible."

There was a further barrage of questions from people, more than could be made sense of. Christian's terror was rapidly turning to annoyance. He was a God-fearing man and devout Methodist. He was simply unaccustomed to not being believed. He could not recall speaking a lie ever before and now he seemed to be on trial for saying what he had just seen. He became indignant.

"Don't believe me eh? Well, outside all of you that think that I am not speaking the God's truth. Further down the pathway you go. See the thing for yourselves. That'll convince you"

Christian Mayweather's challenge was met with a stunned silence. Faced with the reality of putting their objections to the test, suddenly the doubters were not so resolute. People looked at each for somebody to take the lead. Alas, there was no natural leader in the pub that evening.

"Well?" he challenged the crowd.

There were murmurings of embarrassment at their own lack of initiative or bravery in the circumstances. The impasse made it possible for people to contemplate the occurrence. What if it were true?

"What do we do? That thing is out there. What does it want?"

Christian couldn't see who asked the question, but he was quick to answer.

"Whatever it wants, I don't want to find out. I'm not leaving here tonight without a crowd of people around me. And if I make it home safely tonight; I'll be sure to lock the door and bar the windows for fear of whatever it is that is lurking here in the forest."

Again, there was a silence as Christian's words were silently contemplated. The once sleepy township of Matlock now seemed to hold a frightening menace that could barely be considered.

***

Unaware of what had transpired earlier in the evening at the Cricketer's Bat, Martha and Michael Morrell were once more retiring for the night in the stately Balmoral House. It wasn't long before they were both fast asleep.

Martha didn't quite realise it at the time, but a vision was making itself known to her as a dream. She was floating along the pathway where she had seen Alice only a month before. But this time there was a mist veiling everything. If she squinted, Martha could see the shapes of trees and bushes and even the pathway itself.

Something moved on the trail, it caught her eye. It was a man. He was dressed in typical workers clothes, wearing a not-too-flamboyant hat, and making his way as best as he could along the pathway, given the poor light. Martha floated above the man just behind him. She was content to simply follow him along as a silent and unobserved companion on his journey.

There was nothing unusual about this scene, she thought. But in the peripheral of her vision Martha could see a glow. If she concentrated she could make out that it was green in colour. Being a disembodied spirit as she was, she could not manage to turn her head to investigate the glow. It was at the bottom of her vision. In relation to the man walking in her sights it would be some way behind him.

There was a sense of unease now. What was causing this glow? The mist and the poor light and the fact that she had no control over what she was looking at prevented her from investigating, and therefore knowing what it was.

The green glow increased, it seemed to be gaining ground on the man. The man was proceeding with trepidation. It was dark so clearly, he did not want to accidentally leave the path. That could be disastrous in this section of the walking track. Martha recognised the section of the tail. There were some cliff faces just ahead. If you stumbled off the pathway, then certain doom could easily await you.

She moved in closer to the man. He stopped and seemed to be gaining his bearings. Martha thought that she recognised him. He certainly seemed familiar; but exactly who was it?

Then she saw it? A hideous apparition. It was glowing green and lighting the mist that surrounded it. The thing had almost no shape of its own other than approximating the height of the man that it was pursuing. There were many feelers along the side of what could grotesquely be called a body. Too many to count. It was without doubt the most disgusting thing that Martha had ever seen.

The man, alerted by something that Martha did not perceive, turned around and sighted the creature. He ran.

Then nothingness enveloped Martha. She was nowhere. There was no sky, or ground, or anything. It was incredibly peaceful after the horror that she had just witnessed.

Something ahead of her caught Martha's attention. From the nothingness in front of her something was forming. It swirled and coalesced. Then it took form. Alice Athalia stood before Martha.

Martha was overjoyed to see her sister once more.

"Alice, my dear, thank goodness you are here; I just saw the most hideous apparition".

Alice nodded but did not say a word.

"Tell me Alice, what was it? What does it want? Why is it here?"

Martha's questions went unanswered leaving here perplexed.

“Please Alice, I must know. Are we threatened by this thing, whatever it is? How may we protect ourselves from it?”

Again, Martha’s questions went without reply. This prompted Martha to scrutinise her sister more closely.

“Alice are you able to communicate with me?”

Alice shook her head, a look of absolute desolation on her face. It was not the response that Martha wanted. This was just like before. Alice for some reason from beyond the grave would not, or more likely could not speak to her. Martha’s mind raced. She needed to make the most of this communion with Alice. She did not know when it would come to an end.

“That thing that I saw; it is real and it is here with us in Matlock now?”

Alice nodded. Martha, contemplated her next question. It had to give her the maximum amount of information with the minimum amount of response from her sister.

“Have you encountered this beast before?”

Alice nodded, clearly pleased with her sister’s line of questioning.

“Was it in London?” Martha couldn’t help the note of dismay creeping into her voice.

Alice nodded again. A sudden thought struck Martha. It struck at the very core of her being.

“Alice my dear; was this monster responsible for your death?”

Even as Martha asked the question, she dreaded the reply. Alice nodded. Martha felt a pang of grief well up within her. If she had been not so distracted by the shock of the information Martha may have noticed what Alice was doing now. Alice was pointing furiously at Martha. Over and over she pointed at herself and then at Martha. But grief-stricken now, Martha did not understand the reference. If she had, she may have interpreted it as a warning. The creature that had been responsible for Alice's death will soon have Martha clearly in its inhuman sights.

Chapter 6: Martha Morrell and Christian Mayweather

Martha work with a fright. The memory of the dream still fresh in her mind. Michael was breathing heavily beside her. Not quite snoring, but not breathing quietly either. Her sudden awakening had not disturbed him at all. She lay awake for quite some time pondering what to do.

Her thoughts turned to the man that was pursued by the creature. Did he escape? She desperately hoped so. Alice had given her information from beyond the grave that people needed to know. They were all in danger from a monster of some description, from goodness knows where? It was up to Martha Morrell to ensure that everybody knew it.

***

Martha had eventually been able to sleep once more. But upon waking at her usual time and preparing breakfast for Michael and herself, she had insisted that they walk into town to meet with the Mayor. Michael was initially perplexed at the idea. But Martha told him that she would explain on the way into town. And that is exactly what she did.

The walk into Matlock, given their advanced ages, took just over an hour. More than enough time for Martha to explain the dream-warning from Alice. He took the news rather badly.

"That would mean that the *thing* that Albert Brawnly saw as real and it may very well have been responsible for his death." He was aggrieved at not giving Albert the benefit of the doubt. But it was too late now. Martha consoled him.

"We need to concentrate on the living now Michael. It is our duty to warn the townspeople of this menace; we don't know when it will strike again"

Michael was comforted by the thought, in an odd way. He agreed. They had reached the town hall by now and were surprised to find none-other than Christian Mayweather on the main external steps addressing a crowd that had gathered. The mayor was beside him. They joined the throng of people to listen to what was being said. Someone in the crowd prompted Christian.

"Tell us again, what *exactly* was it that you saw?"

There was a noise of agreement from the crowd.

"I will tell you. I was walking back from visiting old man Mallory. Lives by himself he does and needs a hand with things nowadays. It was dark. I was alone on the track that leads from Mallory's cottage, past the Cricketer's Bat Inn and then onwards to my cottage. Then I saw it…." He paused for dramatic effect.

"Green and large, big as me it was. Moved across the ground without feet, without legs, but it moved anyway. No face that I could see. No arms, hands nothing recognisable as a man. Came at me though the mist it did."

People were gasping, enthralled by the story and the passion with which it was being told.

"Unholy daemon of some description searching for a soul to feast upon"

Christian's words were frightening to the crowd who reacted accordingly. It was too much for the mayor who intervened at this point.

"Oh, really mister Mayweather; how could you possibly know that it was after your immortal soul? Did it say as much?" Thaddeus's tone was replete with scorn. All of it lost on Christian who brushed it aside.

"You all know me" he said pointing dramatically at the audience.

"You know me to be a God-fearing man. Always walked on the straight-and-narrow I have; for my whole life. No evil booze, no gambling, no wonton carnal desires. So, I know. *I know* what it was after. It was after my soul. Spawn from old nick himself. That must be what it was."

Christian's words shocked the crowd who erupted with calls of fear and alarm. The mayor almost slapped his forehead in frustration. Managing this circus was becoming unbearable.

Martha took it upon herself to interject at this point.

"He is right" she pointed directly at Christian Mayweather. People stopped their calls for protection and help to the mayor and turned to see who was speaking.

“Mister Mayweather is correct. Again, I have had a vision of my deceased sister Madam Alice Athalia. Again, she has warned me about this monster that lurks amongst the tress of Matlock. Just as I told you at poor Albert Brawnly’s funeral. It *is* real, and we are in danger. Each and every one of us!”

Martha’s words made the crowd erupt in pandemonium.

In the crowd there were the business owners that had met previously and decided to take action to diffuse this rumour. Now they were all looking at each other unsure of what to think or do.

From his vantage point on the steps, Thaddeus Tremorlund could see the unravelling of his previous work. He could see the indecision and worry on the spa owner’s faces, one and all. All of the careful direction that he and his town leaders had set had come asunder. Bad news always spread in a town much faster than good. He dreaded the thought of this news permeating his town like the black-plague.

It was some time before he could restore order to the melee.

“Enough please, please calm down, we will achieve nothing by panicking.!” His raised tone eventually prevailed. People were ready to listen to him again.

“Missus Morrell; thank you very much for your insights, but please spare us your nightmares. It is hard enough to contemplate that this so-called monster exists at all without you adding fuel to a fire that may very well, and more than likely be nothing more than…..”

He had everybody's attention. All eyes were focussed upon him. But then he realised that he did not have an explanation for what Christian Mayweather had seen. His mind raced. He had to say something; but what? The pause had gone on for too long. People were visibly restless again.

"Nothing more than what Thaddeus?" someone from the crowd shouted.

"A prank" Even as the mayor spoke the words he did not seem to believe them. But he had no other logical explanation. He seized upon the only one that made any sense and elaborated.

"That is what it must be, a silly prank designed by somebody to....for their own nefarious reasons and purposes. It simply could not be anything else."

Thaddeus tried as best as he could to sound and look completely confident. He could see some members of the crowd nodding in agreement. It elicited more conversation within the audience.

Martha however, would not be silenced so easily.

"When one receives a warning from beyond the grave, it is unwise to ignore it Thaddeus!"

Her tone could easily have been a school teacher correcting an errant child. This too met with agreement with some of the people. Mayor Tremorlund squinted and tried not to roll his eyes in frustration. It would not be seemly to show such emotion in this instance. He needed to maintain his viewpoint and transfer it to the people of Matlock somehow. The only way to do that was to be persistent.

"Martha, I will not belittle your beliefs even if they are not my own. But I will caution you that your viewpoint is prompting unrest in our peaceful little town. I am sure that that is not your intention."

He was wrong in hoping that he could appeal to Martha Morrells sense of township community.

"I have the best interests of everybody here when I tell you that we are in danger and we need to protect ourselves from this monster!"

Martha's words stimulated fear and loud debate from the people once more. Thaddeus could see that he was going to lose this battle if he did not wrest victory from the jaws of defeat soon. He gestured to the people to calm down.

"My friends, please calm yourselves." He needed to end this shambolic impromptu town meeting as quickly as he could.

"I for one will not be swayed by anything other than absolute fact!" He shouted with such ferocity that he garnered everyone's attention. Pleased with the effect that he had, he sought to expand upon his success.

"Nobody here can tell me with hand on their hearts that this is not a childish prank of some sort by person or persons unknown for their own ridiculous reasons. And until I am faced with undeniable fact, I will not be beguiled by the vapours and nuances of other-worldly mumbo-jumbo!"

The mayor gave the crowd a look of defiance, as if to dare them to give him the proof that he demanded.

"I know what I saw Thaddeus" Christian Mayweather spoke once more.

But next to the passionate plea of Mayor Tremorlund it was pale by comparison. Martha could tell that the people were divided. She needed to give them something more than her recounting of a message from her dead sister.

"Christian, come over to Balmoral House when the time is right, and we will hold a séance and contact Alice together. We will ask her for guidance. We will have her point to where we may obtain proof that this danger exists and how we are to combat it."

This met with a murmur of approval from the crowd. It seemed that the next move was with Christian Mayweather. But it was not easy for him to accept such things. He was a devout Methodist and had avoided things like soothsayers, premonitions, card-readings and the like. This was something of an anathema to him.

He looked to the mayor who had a distinctly worried look on his face. He pondered for a short time. The crowd were beginning to cajole him for a reply. If he were to pray during the séance then maybe the almighty would send them a message to explain matters. That was the compromise that he decided upon. A mixture of faith and superstition. He nodded.

"I shall Missus Morrell; thank you very much for your kind offer. I will be delighted to join you for a séance tonight"

He did not sound too assured, but his response met with favour from the gathered townsfolk.

"Not tonight Mister Mayweather. The time has to be right. I am not a gifted psychic as my sister was. I need to assure that the stars are aligned. So, for me, that means that it will need to be on the next full moon. And *that* will be on the second of March."

Martha's delayed invitation was finalised. People bean muttering again. Phrases like 'what if it strikes again before then' were being bandied around. But Martha knew her abilities in contacting the dead were not as honed as Alice's had been throughout her life.

It was mandatory that there be a full moon in order for her to achieve a contact with Alice. And even then, she may not succeed. But this was not information that she cared to share with anyone.

As for what happens between now and then, she was tempted to say that they all needed to pray that it did not terrorise them before she had the chance to consult with Madam Athalia. Instead she addressed her husband.

"Come along my dear, we have some shopping to do before returning home." They left with the regal-air of a king and queen; heading in the direction of the market building further down the road from the Town Hall.

Thaddeus looked down into the crowd. He could see the faces of the spa business owners looking at each other, and then back at him.

There was nothing that could be done about the forthcoming séance, but it was clear that none of them were very happy about it. Thaddeus had bought some time between his own demand for proof and bizarrely the delay before the séance could take place. He did not understand it, but was grateful for the respite. In the ensuing time he could once more being to spread a message of common-sense winning over superstition. At least he hoped that he could.

Chapter 7: The Next Eleven Days

A strange dichotomy had arisen in the town. Faced with two sightings of this mysterious thing, there were people that believed that the town was being haunted by something from beyond the grave. But the complete lack of evidence and the fact that nobody else had seen this creature had others believing that the whole thing was some kind of error.

Town life continued as best as can be expected. The main topic of conversation between neighbours and acquaintances was usually the 'creature'. But as the days and nights passed without any further sightings, even this began to be replaced with subject matter more relevant to the daily lives of the townspeople.

***

Job Smith and the forthcoming opening of the cable car tram was at the forefront of people's minds as the month of February drew to a close and the new month of March began. Although Job Smith's own hydrotherapy establishment was a few months away from opening, the tram-car was going to have an inauguration party all of its own. There was talk of hot-air balloon rides, a parade and a fair on the day. It was slated for the 28th of March. This is what people began to look forward to and discuss with much enthusiasm.

Even Mayor Thaddeus Tremorlund had allowed himself the pleasure of forgetting about the monster incidents in the lead up to the tram opening.

Behind closed doors however, the business owners had met and discussed the forthcoming séance. There was nothing that they could think of to dissuade Martha Morrell from contacting her dead sister. The only course of action was to continue doing what they had been doing so far. Whenever the 'séance' was brought up in conversation, they were always quick to dismiss the idea as "hocus-pocus" and brand the very idea of a séance as "lower class". Which was the kind of insult that held much weight with the proud land-owing residents of Matlock.

***

Nevertheless, the days and nights moved inexorably onwards and soon enough it was Thursday the 2nd of March 1893. Once again talk in Matlock turned to the 'creature' and the communing with the dead that would be taking place that night at Balmoral House. There was a sense of anticipation in the cold air of Matlock.

Chapter 8: The Séance

The full-moon shone brightly in the sky above Matlock. Martha Morrell had made all of the preparations needed for the séance. She had the required number of candles lit in the formal dining room, the place where it was to be held. She had cleansed the room with a mixture of salt and cloves. And she had bathed in a fragrant bath of lavender and nutmeg. The idea being that it was to purify her spirit and make it easier for a kindred soul, such as Alice, to find her way to Martha from the other side.

Christian Mayweather had arrived at ten minutes to eight and was escorted to the dining room by Michael Morrell. Missus Elizabeth Lister, the housekeeper employed by Martha and Michael to do the household chores had been drafted as the fourth person. Although she had originally objected, Martha had assured her that it was safe and that she could not simply use anybody as the fourth, it had to be somebody that she trusted. The compliment had sealed the deal and Missus Lister had agreed. She was waiting at her seat in the dining room when Michael entered with Christian.

"Please be seated Mister Mayweather, Martha will be down shortly and we may begin"

He sat, looking uncomfortable and nervous. A fact not lost on either Michael or Elizabeth. The dining table was large. It could easily accommodate ten diners. It appeared however, that they would all be clustered up at one end. The head dining chair which Christian assumed would be inhabited by Martha was empty. But there were four chairs two on each side. The others had been moved away from the table and were at the side of the room. This therefore left 5 chairs addressing the table. It did not make sense to him. A photograph of an old lady was facing them from the head of the table. He did not know who it was, but it did have a passing resemblance to Martha. He assumed that it was an image of Madam Alice Athalia.

"I see that you've noticed the seating situation Mister Mayweather" said Michael.

Mr. Mayweather nodded.

"The head chair is where we expect Alice to appear. We will be sitting on either side of her. Marth and I upon her right side and Missus Lister and yourself on the left-hand side."

His placement next to Elizabeth Lister made more sense now.

"Have you ever done anything like this before?" Christian inquired of Elizabeth.

"Yes, but it was a number of years ago. Martha doesn't normally dabble in such things. Alice was the gifted one of the two of them."

She went on to explain her prior experience.

"Shortly after we received news of Alice's passing back in 1888 Martha attempted to contact her to find out what happened. The Police report had mentioned something about a burglary of her town-home in London and that she had been murdered sleeping in her bed. It was bereft of detail. And the presiding detective apparently eloped with his fiancé to Switzerland never to be heard from again. So, we were practically left in the dark, weren't we Mister Morrell?" She looked to Michael to reinforce her retelling of Alice's untimely death.

"Indeed, so missus Lister. The Police were evasive and unwilling to provide any detail. There was mention of her butler also running off as well as Alice's housekeeper in her Windsor mansion. It was all very odd to say the least." He shook his head to emphasise the frustration.

"Did you succeed in contacting her?" Christian asked nodding toward the photograph. A reply came from the doorway to the dining room readjusting everybody's attention in that direction. It was Martha.

"It was far too soon to contact such a recently departed soul Mister Mayweather. I should have known better but thought that I would at least try. It comes as no surprise that I did not succeed. Tonight however, will be very different I assure you!" Martha took her seat.

"Why do you say that?" inquired Christian.

"Because I have had dreams of her. Alice *wants* to be summoned. She has a message for us all; and it is up to us to give her the opportunity to do so."

That appeared to be the final word on the matter of why they were convening a séance.

They were all in place now. Martha beside Michael on the right-hand side of the empty chair at the head of the table. And Elizabeth and Christian opposite them. Martha issued her instructions.

“Place the palms of your hands flat against the tablecloth and tilt your heads back. Keep the image of Alice in your minds. I have a photograph there for you to reference Mister Mayweather.”

He indicated that he understood and they all complied. It was quiet. The wind blowing around the sharp stone corners of Balmoral house could be clearly heard. It was somehow unsettling. With only the multitude of candles in the room, the light and shadows played tricks on the closed eyes. Patterns could be seen that took shape into unsettling silhouettes.

“Now, concentrate upon the image of Alice, keep if firmly in your mind’s-eye.”

Martha’s words seemed to come from all around the room.

“We are seeking commune with one that has passed-over. Spirits of the ethereal plain bring us the immortal soul of Alice Athalia, my beloved sister.”

As if Christian’s nerves weren’t frayed enough, the words when spoken sent a shiver through his body. He didn’t know it at the time, but it was repeated in his three companions as well.

“Alice, can you hear me, it is I, Martha. Come through Alice please come through to our world, we beseech you. Tell us what troubles you?”

There was a noticeable temperature drop in the room. Candles began to flicker wildly as if disturbed by an open window. From the head of the table a voice could be heard. It was soft and gentle, but ripped into their consciousness like a hot blade.

“Martha”

Everybody’s eyes sprang open. Alice Athalia was sitting at the head of the table. Elizabeth and Christian audibly gulped and drew-in breath sharply, but resisted crying out. Even Michael was shocked, he could feel his heart beating faster. Only Martha seemed unfazed by the apparition seated with them.

“Alice, my dear, thank you for coming. I have missed you so!” Martha’s passion was evident.

Alice looked furtively to one side off into the shadowed corner of the room as if listening to something.

“What is it Alice?” inquired Martha, clearly worried.

“I have to warn you Martha, the creature that you have seen in your dreams, the one that murdered me in London...........” Alice’s lips were still moving but the remainder of the words could not be heard.

“What was that Alice, I could not hear the last part of that sentence? What about the creature?” Martha prompted her sister to repeat her unheard words.

Alice seemed to flicker as wildly as the candles around the room. She vanished for a second and then reappeared. She began to speak again, but frustratingly the words could not be heard.

"Alice we cannot hear you" pleaded Martha.

Alice once more looked over to where there was nothing but a darkened corner. She tried to speak, this time it was audible.

"It is real Martha, it is here in Matlock and it can………" again the entire warning could not be heard.

"It can what Alice? Please tell us" Martha's frustration apparent.

Perhaps realising that she could not vocalise a complete warning, Alice began to gesture toward her face. It looked as if she was mimicking putting on a mask for a masquerade ball and the swapping it for another one. It did not make any sense to Christian, or Elizabeth or Michael. But Martha was quicker to prescribe a meaning to it.

"It wants to eat people's faces?" It was a guess, but given the circumstances, as ridiculous as it sounded, it was at least a starting point.

Alice shook her head and repeated the charade.

"You are imitating the creature?" posed Martha. Alice nodded.

"The creature is able to change its face?" she further conjectured. Alice looked pleased and nodded enthusiastically.

"Oh, dear Lord above; are you telling us that this creature can look like one of us, like *any* one of us!?"

"Yes" replied Alice, able to be heard once more. "Trust nobody Martha it could be any one of the townsfolk….." Alice's words trailed off into silence once more. The lighting in the dining room flickered wildly and the image of Alice imitated them. One second she was there, the next she was gone only to return and disappear over and over.

"The Miners, I can see their future, Martha, you must warn them.."

The reference came as a complete surprise to all of them. Miners? It took a little while of one looking to the other to interpret what Alice was referring to. She had once more flickered into nothingness.

"The coal mine at Rowsley?" offered Christian.

"Too far away. Surely it must be something closer to Matlock" replied Michael.

"The Matlockite mine at Starkholmes! That is practically on the doorstep of Matlock" offered Elizabeth.

"Yes, that must be it, thank you Missus Lister" Martha, and the rest were again waiting for Alice to re-appear; and she did. Her lips were moving. There was more that she wanted to impart to the gathered people but it was no good. As if a line had been crossed, or an unimaginable timeframe exceeded, Alice was gone.

"No!" shouted Martha.

“Everybody, close your eyes and think of Alice. We must get her back!”

Nobody dared to question or not comply immediately.

“Alice, we are here. Let our lives be the guiding-light to bring you back to us. What more do you have to tell us dear sister, please help us in our need?”

But it was no good. And try as she might over the next ten or fifteen minutes, Alice could not be made to appear once more to them. Eventually Martha succumbed to defeat.

“She is gone.” Her tone desolate.

“It is real and it is here and it can look like any one of us. That is all of the information that we need Martha” Michael’s logical summation brought them all back to the present.

“We need to warn everybody, it is our duty.” Michael’s sense of bravado helped lift the mood in the room. In spite of being faced with the fact that they were being haunted by a creature of unknown origin, they all believed that they had an obligation to warn everyone in Matlock about the danger.

“And it was responsible for her death!” Elizabeth repeated the pertinent fact that could so easily have been obfuscated by the message of doom. It touched Martha.

“Alice may still be alive but for that thing?”

It was an impossible question to answer. Nobody dared.

Christian and Elizabeth were visibly shaking. It was the first time that Martha noticed. She felt sympathy for them. Such things as a successful séance were not the purview of a simple country folk like those here in Matlock.

"I would not have either of you leave the house after such an unsettling evening. And now that we know that that....*thing* is out there, even more so. Michael and I insist that you stay with us for the night. You may journey home in the safely of daylight tomorrow."

Martha's offer was too good to refuse. Balmoral House was a substantial residence. There were many guest rooms. Both of them jumped at the opportunity to take sanctuary within its thick stone walls.

"Thank you misses Morrell" said Elizabeth and the sentiment was echoed with equal zeal by Christian Mayweather. They would take refuge here tonight to ponder the happenings of the bizarre evening and contemplate what to do next.

***

Upon ensuring that their house-guests were comfortable, Martha advised Michael to go to bed. She would spend some time in the kitchen, at the small table writing a letter to the Mayor warning him of the danger that Matlock faced. Gathering her thoughts together she put ink to paper.

To His Worship Thaddeus Tremorlund.

I write to you with news of dire consequence for the people and town of Matlock.

This evening, I have communed with my deceased sister Madam Alice Athalia; famous psychic and advisor to the crowned heads of Europe.

Madam Athalia has given a clear warning that the purported creature sighted first by the late Mister Albert Brawnly and more recently by devout Methodist, Mister Christian Mayweather, is indeed real and a threat to the inhabitants of Matlock.

This warning cannot be ignored.

As Mayor of our fair town, it is your duty to suitably warn the townsfolk of this danger and put into place the necessary actions to hunt and eradicate this menace.

But, be further cautioned that this creature can imitate a person. It has an ability to change faces and become like us. I appreciate how terrifying this news is. A posse of only the bravest and most trustworthy should be convened and made aware of these facts.

I am able to point you in the direction of the Matlockite mine just outside of Starkholmes. My sister has had a vision of the future and wants to warn the miners that they are in imminent danger. This should be your immediate priority upon receipt of this letter.

Madam Athalia's visions of the future are infallible. I use the word with meticulousness. No vision that Alice has seen has ever failed to come to pass.

I trust that the people of Matlock and I can rely upon your immediate action to keep us all safe from this threat to our lives.

Yours Sincerely
Missus Martha Morrell

She dated the letter and read it back to herself a number of times. It was not overstating the gravity of the situation, nor was it understating it. Happy that it would be enough to provoke the Mayor into action, Martha neatly folded it and placed it into an envelope; addressing it accordingly. Now she too felt that it was time for bed.

Chapter 9: Friday the 3rd of March 1893

It would have been easy to guess that neither Elizabeth Lister nor Christian Mayweather slept very well during the night. But eventually sleep overtook them and the next thing they knew, it was morning.

***

Elizabeth set herself the task of making breakfast for everyone, even though the Morrells usually did that for themselves. But a big English breakfast seemed to be the very thing needed to chase away the ghosts of the previous evening. And it worked a treat. Within a few minutes of tucking into the bacon, eggs, toast and beans, and with the sun shining on a beautiful Derbyshire day, the fear of the previous evening receded into memory.

During breakfast Martha presented Christian with the hand-written letter to the Mayor warning him about what they had learned from her dead sister. He agreed to deliver it himself into the hands of the mayor.

Armed with a full stomach both Elizabeth and Christian bid their hosts a good morning and departed with the Morrells waving goodbye from the large oak door. Christian and Elizabeth said their own goodbyes at the front gate because

Missus Lister lived in the opposite direction to Mister Mayweather. They parted and went their separate ways.

Faced with quite a walk into Matlock, Christian did sense his nervousness beginning to gather once more. However, the brilliance of the day soon chased his fears away. He walked confidently down the hillside toward the town.

***

He had been walking for about half an hour when he came to the point where he had initially seen the creature. Although he had passed a couple of early risers on the way, the track was now eerily deserted. He had passed the Cricketer's Bat, which of course was closed given the early hour of the day. He had also passed by the cliff-face where poor Mister Albert Brawnly had met with his tragic fate.

The combination of the recent dreadful happenings, the geographic area and the absence of anyone, had served Christian with another stomach-full of unease. As if that wasn't enough, the brightness of the day had begun to be hampered with the odd occasional thick patch of morning fog. It was prevalent here in the mid ranges of the heights of Matlock, there was none of it up at Balmoral House, from whence he began his journey.

Nevertheless, with his mission to deliver the letter to the Mayor he pushed onwards. It wasn't long before he found himself enshrouded in fog. This heightened his anxiety even more. He moved forward and a natural break in the fog revealed the very thing that he dreaded the most.

The creature was directly in front of him. Christian let out a loud cry. He barely had time to take in the fact that the gelatinous blob was different somehow to the first time that he had encountered it. It was more upright. More like the shape of a person, but without any human features like face or fingers. But he did not care, he spun around with break-neck speed and ran in the opposite direction.

With his heart pounding and his breath depleted from screaming, he ran and ran. Dragging as much air into his lungs as he could he thought to cry out for help once more. Surely the inn keeper from the Cricketer's Bat would hear him?

Any thoughts of help were soon destroyed by the backwards glance that he chanced at the monster. Horrifyingly the creature had formed what looked like human legs covered in black trousers and shoes covering feet. As if that wasn't terrifying enough, the thing was using the legs to pursue him.

Christian almost vomited with fear as he redoubled his efforts to escape from the gruesome thing. At this stage he was so panicked that he couldn't remember if he had called out for help or not. In fact, he had done so a few times, but fear had squashed his ability to concentrate on anything other than trying to escape this nightmare turned real.

Another glance backwards intensified his panic as he realised that the monster was gaining ground on him. Without realising it he let out another holler and drew upon every ounce of his strength to run even faster than before. He couldn't even remember passing the Inn. But now he was back on the track and trees were surrounding him amplifying his dread to a new level of terror.

Branches brushed past his face and he wildly tore at them with his flailing hands and arms. There was a break in the foliage. This was the area where the trail came closest to the cliff-face. Thoughts of Albert Brawnly's untimely demise did not enter his head in the current situation. All thoughts were blotted from his mind as he tripped and fell face-first into the moist ground.

He would not have thought it possible to be even more terrified that he was, and yet, he panicked so totally that he lost all sense of reason. Clambering to his feet he was just able to glance at his foot and realise that it was a tentacle from the creature that had tripped him. He screamed. The thing was almost upon him. But somehow in the effort to regain his stance the tentacle had become untangled from his ankle.

He stumbled again in his efforts to retreat from the monster, but this time it was the uneven surface that foiled his attempt to escape. He was aware that the creature was close. Christian could almost not bring himself to look at it. But he couldn't not look at it. He needed to find a way to get away from the thing.

The blob, for its part had separated into two. The complete unexpectedness of the occurrence focussed Christian's attention totally upon it. Each of the two creatures was about half the size of the original, and yet every bit as horrifying as the whole full-sized monster. He saw the two parts of it once more divide so that now there were four. Proportionally, they were each one quarter of the size of the original. Each of the four formed legs like that of a grotesque child. Each would be capable of pursuing him.

Reason had abandoned Christian Mayweather. If he had been able to employ reason he may have surmised that he, with his legs, could now out-run the menace. But that logic was smothered by the need to find a way to escape. The four monsters had formed a semi-circle around him. He stumbled backward as they advanced upon him.

He looked behind him. The monsters had corralled him so that his back was to the cliff-face. There was no escape. He screamed with all of his might. Only a few more feet and he would be out of ground. He backed up even more. The miniature creatures advanced, menacingly, slowly. He was now at the cliff-edge. He looked down at the dizzying descent.

When he returned his attention to the creatures, they had formed multiple tentacles between them creating a living fence. He was trapped. Although small they were too tall to jump over. Were they? He entertained the thought of a second before it was dashed. The things grew somehow and became thin but taller.

There was noise, a bubbling, gurgling emanating from the things. It was too much for Christian. He couldn't face it anymore. With his heart beating so hard as to reach failure at any second, he turned and hurled himself into space, plummeting downwards to the ground far below.

Any fear that he felt as he fell, was bizarrely less substantial that the fear that he had so effectively just escaped from. The letter that Martha had written to the mayor, tucked neatly into the side pocket of his jacket came loose and fluttered away in the fog and breeze. He clutched at anything that he could as he flew downwards adjacent to the cliff-face. Screaming; Christian Mayweather fell to his death, the impact upon the ground bringing silence to the countryside once more.

***

The monster had coalesced itself into a single form. The featureless face became that of a person. The body, a fully clothed individual. It was nobody that would have been recognized by any of the Matlock inhabitants. He looked at the twisted body of Christian Mayweather far below. A snide smirk covered his face. He enjoyed the terror that he had inflicted upon the man before he had died.

It gave him great pleasure to strike so much fear into somebody that they would hurl themselves from a cliff rather than face him. The only regret that the man-creature had was that he would not now be able to feast upon any of the organs of his victim. It was a long way to reach the part of ground where his intended meal had come to rest. The fog patches were lifting, the sun was shining. He was smart. He knew that the body would be found before he could make use of it. Especially after the noise that he had exuded upon his deathly fall. There must be ramblers around that had heard it.

No matter, there are others that would satisfy his hunger. And he knew exactly where to go in order to fulfil his malevolent desires.

Chapter 10: Noon

Keith Smedley regarded Balmoral House from the front gate. It was very grand indeed for just two people, he thought. The gardens had a look of not quite being cared for enough though. In fact, the entire house looked like it could do with a good cleaning up. Probably built as the trophy for a successfully lived career and then it turned out to be too much to upkeep.

He opened the squeaky gate and made his way up to the grandiose front door. There was a knocker rather than a bell, which surprised Smedley. Given that Michael and Martha had lived in London before retiring here to Matlock, he would have expected the very city townhouse feature of a bell rather than a simple country door knocker. He wondered why they had not had one installed. He made due with the knocker and announced his presence.

It wasn't long before the door was answered by Michael Morrell.

"Good morning mister Morrell" said Smedley smiling.

"Good morning mister Smedley" replied Michael with a tone that seemed to indicate that he was somewhat taken aback by the visitation of a Matlock spa manager.

"I wondered if I may come in and speak with your good wife Mister Morrell?" he said by way of explanation.

The reason for the visit by Keith Smedley suddenly became very clear to Michael. He nodded and moved to allow entry for the visitor.

"Surely; please come in"

Keith took off his hat and entered the rather stately hallway. It was just as splendid as he thought that it would be. Long and wide with a lovely staircase ascending no-doubt to the bedrooms upstairs. Either side of the hallway were doors, one would surely lead to the main reception room. Michael closed the door with a thud and directed Keith to the sitting room on the right.

This too was an impressive sight. High ceilings, walls covered with portrait paintings and various vases that all looked expensive placed here and there. The furniture was stately and inhabited the space nicely.

"Please take a seat and I will fetch Martha" said Michael. But, no sooner had he uttered the words than Martha's voice could be heard from the doorway to the sitting room.

"I am here Michael; good day mister Smedley. To what do we owe the pleasure of your visit today?" Martha entered the room wearing the air of quiet confidence. She moved to stand opposite him and indicated that he should sit. Michael took his place beside his wife.

"I was…..wondering…about your séance last night missus Morrell and wanted to see if there were any…………insights to be gained?" Keith stumbled his way through his question.

Martha frowned slightly.

"You're not here to discuss the letter that I sent the Mayor?" she asked

Keith looked puzzled and slightly shook his head.

"Letter?" he said; at a bit of a loss as to the reference that Martha had made.

"Yes, the séance last night revealed a lot about the danger that we are all in mister Smedley. I wrote a letter to Mayor Tremorlund explaining this. I assumed that is why you came; to discuss it."

"I'm sorry missus Morrell, I know nothing of the letter. I have spoken with the Mayor only an hour ago. I'm sure that he would have mentioned it." Keith explained.

Martha's frown turned to puzzlement and then outright worry.

"What could have happened to mister Mayweather. I charged him with the delivery of the letter. He spent the night as our guest, unwilling, as you can imagine, to travel through the night. But he left at around eight o'clock this morning. He has had more than enough time to walk into Matlock and present the letter to the Mayor."

Michael echoed his wife's sentiments.

"Yes indeed. What could have become of him? This is very concerning!"

Keith could see that both were vexed with the proposition of the missing letter and more importantly the whereabouts of Christian Mayweather. Their ponderings were cut short by the sound of the front door opening and closing. They didn't have to wait long to see who it was that had so abruptly entered unannounced. It was missus Lister, and she was in quite a state.

“Have you heard?!” she practically shouted at them as she scurried into the room.

The look of puzzlement from the people sitting there was all of the reply that Elizabeth needed.

“Christian Mayweather, found dead in the same spot as Albert Brawnly!” she blurted out the shocking news. Martha and Keith stood up. Both spoke over the top of each other.

“What; when?!”

“That’s terrible!”

“I’m shaking like a leaf” was the only reply that they received from missus Lister.

“My poor dear, here come sit down; Michael a sherry for missus Lister please.” Martha attempted to take control of the situation and restore the orderly calm that was the usual pervasiveness in Balmoral House. Elizabeth Lister took a seat beside Martha has she was instructed, clearly relieved to be off her feet. Michael had moved to a nearby cabinet and opened it to reveal various bottles. He picked up one removed the glass stopper and poured a small glass of Sherry. He handed it to Elizabeth when he returned to the sofa.

“Bless you mister Morrell” she said and unceremoniously gulped it down in one mouthful. Martha relieved Elizabeth of the glass and indicated to Michael that perhaps he had better refill it.

“Tell us everything that you know” directed Martha.

Elizabeth seemed to collect her thoughts and then began to speak. Slowly at first and then gathering momentum as she proceeded.

"After we both left this morning, mister Mayweather and me, we went our separate ways. He took the track that goes into town and I went in the opposite direction to go home. David comes home today from his three weeks shift up north; he works for the railways you know."

Keith assumed correctly, that this must be missus Lister's husband. She continued.

"No sooner had he walked in the door than he tells me that he had heard that someone had died here in Matlock, this very morning. Well, I was horrified, I mean who wouldn't be? But he didn't know who it was. So, we set about trying to find out who it was. I hurried through cooking him a late breakfast. Hungry he was, after travelling home from up north. Then, we set out to the local shop to see if they knew anything. Well, they had heard the same news but didn't know either."

Elizabeth's retelling of how she found out about the tragic fate of Christian Mayweather was in danger of becoming a tedious rant.

"So, we moved on to the next nearest shop, you know the one, further down the hill it is. Well the shopkeeper there, mister Shrewford, told us. It was Christian Mayweather found at the bottom of the cliff. The very same one that had taken the life of Albert Brawnly. What does it all mean? How could this have happened? Why weren't we warned in the séance last night? This is terrible, a terrible thing!" Elizabeth began to sob.

"There, there misses Lister. Perhaps Alice did warn us, but we did not have the ears to hear." She presented Elizabeth with the refilled glass of Sherry.

It was a small comfort in the face of news of such heartbreaking misfortune.

"I assume that the body has been taken to the morgue?" Keith spoke up.

Elizabeth gave him a curious look as if only now realising that he was there.

"Mister Smedley; why are you here?" her rather blunt question hung in the air.

"I was hoping to find out more about the séance last night. Christian Mayweather was here last night, for the séance?" he sought affirmation of what had already been established.

"Yes" replied Michael.

"And you managed to contact your deceased sister, Madam Athalia?" he further inquired.

"Could see her as plain as I see you know!" chipped in Elizabeth.

"Why weren't you warned in the séance last night" Keith reiterated the earlier distressed words of Elizabeth, but posed them as a question that required an answer.

Martha could see that Keith Smedley was inquisitive, but not dismissive. It pleased her to answer him then in some detail.

“Mister Smedley, my sister did give us ample warning of the creature that lurks in the forest surrounding Matlock. It *is* real. And furthermore, there was a clear warning for the miners that work just south of the town. But more importantly is the news that this creature can assume the face of any of us. It can hide effectively beneath our very noses, and none of us would be any the wiser.”

Martha finished her brief summation of the contents of the séance and waited for a reaction from the prominent business-owner.

For his part, Keith Smedley listened to what Martha was saying with a look of concentration painted upon his features. He then contemplated what was said. It was difficult to know from his poker-face exactly what was going through his mind. Martha, Michael and Elizabeth waited for the next words from Keith.

“Missus Morrell, I think that in the face of the prevailing circumstances, one sighting of this monster could be considered imaginary. And then to result in death; that too could be counted as sheer happenstance. But two sightings of the Monster of Matlock? And then for that man too, the one that had witnessed the creature, to die in exactly the same way, in exactly the same spot? That is surely far more than coincidental!”

Keith Smedley’s summing up of the situation that they found themselves in, brought a shiver to them all, including

Smedley. There were a few moments of silent contemplation. Then, Keith held missus Morrells gaze and said.

"I think that you had best tell me everything that happened in the séance last night".

Chapter 11: Matlock Town Hall

It was about two o'clock in the afternoon when Keith Smedley made it to town. He could have been there much sooner but chose to spend time with Martha, Michael and Elizabeth going over in detail everything that had happened at the séance. He pulled his bicycle up to the steps of the Town Hall. Even here he could see that there was commotion above and beyond the usual. People were gathered in small groups here and there. And he could tell that they weren't discussing some civic work, or even the forthcoming opening of the cable-car tram. From what he could hear, there was one topic of conversation this sunny Friday afternoon; the untimely death of Christian Mayweather.

He rested his bicycle against the stone balustrade and went up the stairs and inside the building. A similar scene was repeated on the innards of the town hall. People gathered in small groups looked over to see who had entered. He nodded acknowledgement to those that he knew well and strode up to the closed door of the Mayor's office.

He knocked twice and without waiting for a response, entered. Inside Mayor Tremorlund was with Chief Wiksworth and two of his more familiar, and more local Constables by the names of Wilson and Harrison. But there was a fifth man present that he had not seen before.

"Please Mister Smedley, can't you see that I'm in a meeting with Captain Wiksworth?" He was quite gruff.

"I am sorry your Worship, but this cannot wait. It has to do with the very thing that you are surely discussing; Christian Mayweather's death".

This was a different matter entirely. The Mayor had wrongly assumed that it was a business matter of some kind. But now Keith Smedley had the undivided attention of everyone in the room. Keith looked at the man he did not know before speaking. Captain Wiksworth did the honours.

"Mister Sidney Taylor, Derbyshire district Coroner, this is Mister Keith Smedley, manager of Smedley's Hydro.

They shook hands and exchanged pleasantries.

"Now what's all this about Mister Mayweather's death?" prompted Wiksworth.

"I have just come from an in-depth discussion with Martha and Michael Morrell at Balmoral House...." He began, but was immediately and rudely interrupted by the Mayor.

"Oh, Please Mister Smedley! Spare us the rantings of an old woman convinced that she can commune with the dead!"

The revelation brought a new perspective on matters for the Captain and Constables, all of whom gave Smedley a look of warning that this was surely not what he intended to discuss. But Keith would not be swayed.

"Your Worship, two sightings of this purported monster, and both witnesses' dead by falling from the same cliff.

Nobody could possibly believe that there was not much more to this than happenstance!"

Captain Wiksworth entered the argument.

"Indeed, Mister Smedley, a reasonable man would naturally assume that there is more to this than meets the eye, but we can only concern ourselves with facts. Mayor Tremorlund has warned me about the séance supposedly held last night. It would be difficult to not hear somebody in town talking about it. But if the truth behind what has happened is to be uncovered, I do not believe that it will be with a Ouija board."

Smedley could see that he would have to present what he knew with caveats so as to please the doubters in the room. He caught himself thinking that thought. Doubters? He wasn't entirely sure that he wasn't one of them. But Martha, and Michael and Elizabeth were very impassioned with what they told him. It would be difficult not to get caught up in their view of things. He paused for a moment and then began.

"Will you at least do me the courtesy of listening to what they have said. You will be receiving the information directly from them, through me, to you. That must be better than hearing about what happened on the town grape-vine? The information would have been with you this very day in the form of a letter from Martha Morrell; that should have been delivered in person to the Mayor, by Christian Mayweather."

The strategy worked. They were all in agreement with him. And now their curiosity had been piqued by the reference to the letter, undelivered by the deceased. With their collective permission to proceed, he recommenced.

"The warning from Madam Athalia, contacted from beyond the grave by her sister Martha Morell was three-fold. Firstly, the monster is real. It is here, and it is a threat to us all".

This garnered a grumble of either disapproval or concern from the men. It was hard to tell which.

"Secondly, the thing, whatever it is and whatever it wants, has not been seen by many because it is adept at hiding. Hiding in a way that it may very well be in plain sight and we would be unaware. For you see, this creature can look like a man. It can look like any one of us."

This was too much for the men, they erupted with objections of 'preposterous', 'rubbish', and 'utter nonsense'. Smedley realised that perhaps he should have kept that part for the final point. But it was too late. He was in danger of losing their attention completely, so he emphasised that there was only a single remaining message to be heeded.

"Please, everyone. I know how this sounds. But there may be a group of people that can verify that this creature is real!"

The assertion had the attention of everyone in the room once more.

"Well?" prompted the Mayor

"The third message was one directed specifically at the miners in the Matlockite mine just south of the town. Apparently, they featured in the warning from Madam Athalia.

Exactly how is unclear. Nevertheless, I think that it would be prudent to visit them in all haste and see what they know."

It was a reasonable course of action. But the Mayor was having none of it.

"Thank you, Mister Smedley for that amusing reiteration of what I am sure was an Absinthe-driven hallucination from all concerned!"

His dismissive tone and accusation that the séance was predicated upon alcohol was damning enough to wipe away everything that he had just said. Smedley was angry, but he had been given his chance and it appeared that he had failed to convince his audience.

"Facts Mister Smedley, that is what will solve this case, if in fact, there is a case to solve. Remember, that as incredible a coincidence as it was, this may yet be proven to be nothing more than just that." Captain Wiksworth stood his middle-ground on the matter. He turned to the Coroner.

"Would you like to see the body? Doctor Moxton has pronounced death by falling from a great height, and breaking of various vital bones."

"Yes, indeed I would" replied Sidney Taylor.

"May I join you?" Smedley was quick to take the initiative. He did not know exactly what he was hoping to find or achieve. But it seemed the correct thing to do. Then he thought aloud.

"The miners…"

Mayor Tremorlund could be seen to roll his eyes in exasperation. But then paradoxically offered a consolation.

"I will go and see to the welfare of the Miners directly after this meeting. I will ask them if they know anything about a local monster that can masquerade as a man and let you all know the outcome of what I am sure will be a riotous belly laugh of a response from them all".

The unusual offer was seized-upon by Captain Wiksworth.

"Excellent idea Thaddeus, thank you for offering your assistance in this matter. That will free-up my constables to canvas the townsfolk nearby to the scene of the…accident."

A way forward seemed to have been agreed. They all now had missions to accomplish; except for the Captain, but nobody noticed.

"Well I think that we should all be getting on" he said in his officious police Captain's voice.

***

Matlockite is an unremarkable lead halide mineral that was first discovered in the early 1800's. The miner was thinking this very thought about the piece of Matlockite that he was holding. It did not have any practical purpose that anyone had, as yet, discovered. It was not particularly valuable. But it was rare. And in geological circles, that made it worth mining.

There were universities around the world that were writing to Matlock begging for a piece of Matlockite for their geological collections. It did not sell for very much. But the popularity with educational institutions the world over ensured that this mine was able to support a team of six miners.

All were on duty today. It was not difficult to mine, like coal would be. In the case of Matlockite, it was easy to see the seam and follow it, chipping away until sizeable chunks of Matlockite could be extracted from the walls.

The mine had been in operation since about 1850 and still the demand for this inconspicuous mineral was steady. Perhaps he should just be grateful to have a job here in the Matlockite mine rather than in a lung-choking coal mine. The man dismissed his silent musings and threw the chunk of mineral into a waiting bucket.

The mine was not deep underground, it was in the side of a hill, but it was deep in the fact that it went a long way into the hillside. Dynamite had been used to effectively follow the rich seam of Matlockite, gouging a roughly circular man-made cave. Although beam supports had been erected, to ensure no cave-ins, they were almost redundant. The rock in this part of Matlock was hard. The mine was able to support itself.

Unknown to the six men working far inside, the creature entered the mine. As it moved further into the mine the daylight faded. It was able to see in the dark without the assistance of light so it did not care. Inexorably it moved onwards. Its keen senses could detect the men ahead, still quite a way. There was no counter shaft, in this kind of mine there was no need. Meaning, there was no way for the men to escape. Like chickens in the den of a fox, they were doomed.

The abject darkness began to give way to light. Oil lamps lighting the innermost part of the mine. Here is where the men were spending their final moments of life. It moved closer. Soon they would be able to see it.

One of the miners became aware of a dull, green glow. It was coming from the darkened way out of the mine. Oil lamps were not lit for the entire length of the mine. It was easier to carry lamps with each man and then, when agglomerated together, they made more than enough light for the six of them to work by.

He stopped chipping at a particularly dense vein of Matlockite to peer into the gloom. One of his compatriots noticed and asked him what he was doing.

"Wondering what's for tea tonight?' he said jokingly.

His friend responded by peering more intently at the green glow. It looked like it was getting closer.

"What's that?" he said quietly. His friend turned and saw what had vexed the man. It looked like someone was coming toward them carrying an oil lamp that emanated green light. It was rather peculiar.

By this time a third man had seen what was going on and joined in the fold, seeking an explanation for what they were witnessing. He alerted his fellow miners.

"Fellows, look over here, the most unusual thing!"

As he said it, all faces were now turned toward the green light moving toward them through the darkness. As it approached, the light took on the form of a man. All at once the miners perceived that there was a glowing green man walking towards them.

"It's a ghost!" exclaimed one of them.

Chapter 12: Death, Multiplied by Seven

"Keith"

Smedley had no sooner exited the mayor's office when he ran into somebody that he knew; and they had called him by name.

"William; hello" he said by way of greeting, instantly recognising the man.

Then, as the police chief, constables and mayor moved past them, he took the time to introduce the coroner, who had also stopped along with Smedley.

"Mister William Aitkens, owner of the Rockside Hydropathic Establishment, meet Mister Sidney Taylor, the Derbyshire district Coroner."

They were both contemporaries; late forties or early fifties. Each impeccably dressed, and with a finesse of character, easily identified in the men, that could only have come from a well-healed education in their youth.

"It's a pleasure to make your acquaintance" responded Taylor.

"And yours too" said Aitkens. Then he continued, addressing them both.

"Nasty thing this; another death."

"We're just on our way to the morgue now" offered Smedley. Which was not really giving away his current viewpoint that something was definitely amiss.

“I studied anatomy at Edinburgh university” offered Aitkens. He was clearly eager to join them. Smedley looked to the Coroner for his reaction.

“Well, you know what they say, three’s company!” It was a generous offer. If he had been a more officious man, he may have stood upon rules and regulations and not allowed either of the men to accompany him to inspect the body. But thankfully he was not.

“Jolly good show; then, let’s be off” said Aitkens.

The three of them left the town hall and walked in the direction of the hospital.

***

Pandemonium erupted in the mineshaft. Grown men screamed at the top of their lungs. The green shape resolved itself into a man-sized featureless globule of pulsating jelly. It had purpose. It moved with intent. Everything about it was threatening; and it was blocking the only exit.

“RUN!” screamed one of the men. Nobody knew nor cared which. It was a thought that they all had almost simultaneously. But there was nowhere to go. The thing began to change shape. As if its presence wasn’t terrifying enough, now it was changing its appearance. It was wider now. Any thought of taking a chance running past it on either side was scuttled. It now took up the entire width of the mineshaft.

Men screamed even more fiercely. Useless warnings or narratives about the beast were lost.

"It's the devil himself!"

"Oh God help us!"

The men were cowering together at the back of the mine. The more scared ones pushing their way to the back of the pack. The sense of dread was so overwhelming that one of the men began to feint. His eyes rolled up into the back of his head and he fell forward, his body weight slamming him in to the rock floor with a thud. The unconscious body now the closest one to the creature.

The monster shot out tendrils from its longitudinal axis. Fifty or more, it was impossible to tell under the circumstances. The result was a web of tendrils now emanating from the daemon effectively trapping them in a living cage.

Another tendril shot out from the thing. But this one from the front centre of the beast. It latched onto the comatose man and dragged him toward the main body of the blob, separating the cataleptic man from his friends.

Any minute sense of relief that it was not one of them was destroyed as a mouth appeared on the monster somewhere proportionally where the 'head' would have been, if it had one.

The tendril now altered its shape to that of a razor sharp thin and incredibly strong tool that wavered menacingly over the victim and then plunged itself into the gut of the man. The shock woke him from is unconsciousness. He shook and screamed in agony as the scalpel carved a hole into his stomach. He made to scream once more but the tendril had reformed itself into something akin to an octopus tentacle and brutally pushed into the man searching for something.

A muffled gurgle and what looked to be the man's liver was wrenched out. Any connecting organs were pulled out with it. Innards of the man spewed out over the rock floor. It could have been the shock or the sudden loss of vital organs, or more than likely the combination of the two, but the man surrendered to death.

There was stunned silence from the remaining miners. Ominously the liver was flicked around as if taunting the men with it before it was brought up slowly and deliberately to the 'mouth' of the beast who proceeded to eat it whole.

The youngest of the men vomited with a combination of fear and disgust. Others renewed their calls to heaven above for help. None of them knew how much pleasure it was bringing the monster of Matlock to hear their cries of anguish. The perverse organism feeling raptures of delight to see how much agony it was inflicting upon the hapless men.

It had time on its side. There was no need to hurry. Who would be looking for these men here in the bottom of a mineshaft. But it was hungry too. It had been quite some time before it had nourished itself. A thought occurred to the creature. Maybe it should completely absorb one of the men. It could then take on that form. There was plenty of time to decide, it though.

A tentacle began to explore the innards of the fallen man. It found nothing that it wanted. Another volunteer to be eviscerated was required. Mercifully, the men could not hear its thoughts. Their level of terror could have magnified ten-fold, should they have been able to.

The tendril extricated itself from the dead man and wavered before the remaining five. Choosing one at random it flicked forward in an instant latching onto and covering the terrified man's face. He couldn't breathe. He pulled frantically at the jelly-like protrusion that was suffocating him, to no avail. The panic that he felt hastened the man's demise. He convulsed violently multiple times before collapsing to the ground. The creature pulled the body toward itself.

"I can't take it!"

One of the remaining men shouted and unable to think clearly threw himself at the extreme ends of the tendril-web that encapsulated them. The creature's central tentacle that had finished drawing the next man to the main body-mass of the beast let go of the dead man. It re-shaped itself into a long thin sword-like shape and flicked at the man with such a force that it severed the panic-stricken man in two. The top half and bottom half of the man fell in different directions.

It could be seen by the horrified remaining three, that the eyes of the man were still open and looking about in fear; the mouth still uttering something that could not be heard. Like a victim of the French Revolution's guillotine, the man shuddered into motionlessness.

Free to reformulate itself once more, the central tentacle greedily lunged into the torso of the newly fallen man and pulled out the heart. It had a few more beats left to it before it too became still. The heart was ravenously shoved into the creature's waiting mouth. It could be seen to chomp on it a few times before swallowing.

There were no words to describe the fear that enveloped the three men remaining alive. They could see their immediate futures. There was absolutely no hope whatsoever. All three were wailing in desperation. Shaking their heads in denial of what was soon to be unalterable fact.

The beast began to laugh. It emanated a hideous sound that approximated a man's laugh. But the sound was perverted in some way. It made the sound of laughter all the more demon-like, despicable, totally and unconditionally evil.

One of the men had, in desperation, managed to gather enough presence of mind to plead with the beast.

"Oh God, please; no!"

But nothing could dissuade the thing from its irrevocable course of murder and mayhem and frenzy of feeding on the living innards of its victims.

***

Keith Smedley, William Aitkens and Sidney Taylor had arrived at the morgue just as Doctor William Moxton was covering up the body of Christian Mayweather. He was somewhat surprised to see the three men entering the small morgue. Not so much Sidney Taylor, with whom he was professionally-acquainted; but the fact that the District Coroner was accompanied by the Manager of Smedley's Hydro and the owner of Rockside Hydro. In answer to his unasked question the Coroner decided to explain the presence of the other men.

"Nasty business this William; I assume that you know your townsfolk?" he indicated to the two men with him. Doctor Moxton nodded and mumbled a hello of sorts.

"Nothing spreads factual news in a township like the word of men of stature. Wouldn't you agree?" he further asked the physician.

Still looking a little confused and slightly flustered he seemed to begrudgingly agree.

"Well then, having such men at hand is the best course of action then. It is better to have the facts of the matter reiterated in the general populous rather than unsubstantiated rumour and speculation. It will put to rest any such misinformation before it can occur." With his 'logic' now stated he proceeded to get to the heart of the matter.

"What have you found?"

Doctor Moxton was still somewhat vexed but proceeded to report his findings to the Coroner anyway. The Physician complied and pulled back the sheet once more revealing the dead body of Christian Mayweather.

"Death by broken neck, sustained by falling from a great height. Note the contusions here and here and the obvious break in the neck. Various other bruising consistent with falling onto hard ground." Doctor Moxton pointed at the various signs of damage.

"Yes, yes; I see" said the Coroner.

"Not much else to report. A fall for reasons unknown?" Moxton completed his summary.

Keith Smedley noticed something in both clenched hands of the deceased.

"What's in his hands?" he asked. This garnered the attention of all the men. The Doctor reached out and prised open the fingers of one, then the other hand extracting the foliage.

"Leaves he said examining one and handing on the small clutch of others that he had recovered"

They all looked at the green specimens.

"Pyrostegia Venusta" said Smedley

"Eh?" came the triumvirate of non-understanding from the other three.

"Commonly known as the Orange Trumpet Vine or the Flame Vine. A native of Brazil, Argentina, Bolivia and Paraguay."

"What on earth is it doing in rural Derbyshire?" queried Aitkens.

"It must have been brought back by an explorer, or a botanist that thought that it would be interesting. But the thing is it is a pest. We have it growing in the grounds of Smedley's Hydro. Strong as ropes those vines and equally hard to get rid of. I hadn't noticed it in the surrounding countryside. But until it flowers, I suppose that it is just a non-descript vine"

His explanation finished, the other three nodded as if only half interested in the information.

"Not poisonous then?" asked Sidley Taylor, wanting to check-off any possibility of death by another means.

"No" confirmed Smedley. Then he went on to say

"Is there any sign of anything else on his body Doctor. Markings of……" He faded, not sure of how to ask for signs of a Monster.

"Signs of what Mister Smedley?" queried Moxton.

"Anything unusual, anything, out-of-the-ordinary?" he said.

Doctor Moxton looked firstly at the Coroner, as if non-verbally asking for clarification, and when none came looked at William Aitkens. Similarly, he did not elaborate on the point.

"None" he said rather dryly; giving Smedley a slightly irritated look.

"Perhaps if you could be more specific on exactly what you think there may be?"

It looked as if nobody was going to let the Doctor in on the recent discussions in the Mayor's office, but then William Aitkens spoke up.

"Monster markings Doctor; anything that may have been left by something unexplained in nature?"

There was an awkward pause before Doctor Moxton said slowly and deliberately.

"You're not serious?"

There was no reply from any of the men. They looked at each other hoping that one would verify the assertion, but none did.

"You *are* serious?" he said stunned by the query.

"What on earth would I be looking for exactly? Claw marks from winged-predator? Teeth marks from an African lion or maybe a horn wound from a Rhinoceros?" Doctor Moxton's sarcasm left the men in no-doubt as to his disposition on the matter.

"Please Doctor, I know that it sounds fanciful but as the District Coroner, I should leave no stone unturned. Is there anything on the body that suggests that he may have been held first and then hurled from the cliff? Or even fatally injured before he fell?'

It was clear from Doctor Moxton's face that he was not amused by the unusual questioning. But at the same time, he was not prepared to casually dismiss a direct question from the District Coroner.

"No, Sidney, there is absolutely no evidence of anything like that. None at all!" he enforced his answer by glaring at both William and Keith before further stating

"Monster hunting is the fodder of fiction authors like Mary Shelley and Robert Louis Stevenson. Perhaps you'd better stick to botany Mister Smedley?"

Somewhat humbled by the resolve of Doctor Moxton, both Smedley and Aitkens did not pursue the matter any further.

"It looks like there is nothing to support death by any other cause. This will be reported then, as a horrible accident. It appears that there is nothing more to say gentleman." Sidney Taylor summarised for the men, his official report. He left them in absolutely no-doubt as to what the certified stance would be on the tragic death.

Keith looked somewhat dejected, but at the same time, how could he support with evidence the story of the Monster of Matlock if there was none? He wondered if the Mayor had had any more luck with the Miners? Perhaps they had seen the thing and could support the story. One way or the other, people had to be warned that something was very wrong in Matlock.

Chapter 13: The Matlockite Mine

The Mayor approached the entrance of the mine with a good deal of trepidation. He was wondering why he hadn't brought someone with him. Even one of the Town Hall Clerks would have done. Why did he volunteer to do this?

The question was, of course, rhetorical. He wanted to disprove anything and everything to do with the story of a Monster haunting the town of Matlock. He was so incensed with Keith Smedley and his story from that old-bat Martha Morell that he acted to quash any part of it, without first thinking of the consequences. And it was those consequences that he was now facing.

It was quiet. He knew that the mine was very long nowadays. He had been in it before, but that was years ago. It would be much deeper now than it was then. The mine was seen as a part of the brilliance of living in Matlock. The fact that the town had a mineral named after it, that for whatever reason, could not be found elsewhere. So, the Matlockite was mined here and sent all around the world. In effect, putting Matlock in Derbyshire on the international map. And that thought pleased Mayor Thaddeus Tremorlund very much indeed. He was the town official of a very special place.

There was no sign that anything was amiss as he ventured into the mouth of the man-made cave. He leant down and picked up one of the oil lamps that were strewn around just inside the entrance. Finding, and striking a match he trimmed the wick and then held it ahead of him. The illumination did nothing to reveal the inner most depths of the mine. He sighed in resignation. He had got himself into this situation, he now had to see it through.

Gingerly he ventured forward. The lamp cast shadows on the uneven walls. It was eerie. He steeled himself and pushed onwards. Moments turned into minutes. He felt that he had been walking for at least ten. But then admonished himself. He couldn't have been. Reaching for the chain of his watch, he extracted it from his waistcoat and flicked open the casing. He wasn't sure of the exact time that he had reached the mine; but seeing the time passing on the face of the pocket watch reassured him that he had more than likely, only been walking for a few minutes.

Thaddeus renewed his journey with a little more vigour. He increased his pace as his eyes became accustomed to the gloom. With a good few minutes more of walking he began to see a light in the distance. It comforted him. He wanted to reach the miners now more than ever.

A noise coming from behind startled him. He spun around thrusting the lantern forward in an effort to discover the source of the sound. A flicker of movement on the side of one of the walls alerted him. He repositioned the lantern to get a clearer view of it.

Some loose rock had fallen from its place and made the unexpected noise. A little more followed what must have been a previous larger piece, repeating the sound, in miniature. Reassured that he was not being pursued by something sinister, he renewed his journey toward the light. He would never have thought that being with the miners would be so welcome. But now more than ever, he just wanted to get there and assure himself that all was well. He moved forward.

If his mind had not been so distracted with his nervousness he may have questioned why he could not hear any sounds of mining, or indeed even talking. It wasn't long before he was within visual distance of the end of the mine. It was lit with what looked from this distance like five lanterns. The miners were lying around apparently asleep.

Thaddeus was aghast. Those lazy so-and-so's. He thought to surprise them with his official presence and wake up their little daylight slumber party. He increased his pace to a jog. At least as much of a jog as his portly figure would allow. Bounding forward he called out has he reached the snoozing miners.

"What is all of this, then?" he said in a derogatory tone as he arrived at the site of the carnage. He froze almost unable to comprehend what he was seeing. There was blood dripping from the walls. The miners were all here as far as he could tell, but some had been physically ripped into two or three pieces. Innards were exposed. The stench of blood and gizzards filled the claustrophobic space.

He could see some of the faces of the men. They were twisted in terror and agony. It was unbelievably horrible.

Thaddeus thought to scream but instead the contents of his stomach erupted from his mouth with a force that made him convulse violently. The projectile vomit surged forward in two powerful outpourings. Bizarrely none of it touching any part of himself.

He was coughing and spitting and trying to make sense of what had happened. He backed away from the mess that he had made and the human-muddle of carnage. A hundred thoughts raced through his mind. Martha Morell was right. Keith Smedley's Monster must have done this. What else could kill six men with such strength?

His perfect township was doomed. There would be monster-hunters here within the day forming gangs to hunt down and kill the thing. Tourism was doomed, as dead as the miners lying all around him. The healing waters of Matlock would mean nothing. People would stay away from the town, fearing for their lives. In short, the perfect would of Mayor Thaddeus Tremorlund came crashing down around him.

He fell to his knees and began to weep. He couldn't tell how long he had been their crying like a baby, but it seemed like a very long time. All the while he was staring blankly at something that was on the ground before him. And bit by bit, the reality of what he was looking at invaded his consciousness.

He stopped sobbing for long enough to lean forward, somehow now entranced by the object he had been staring at for so long. It was so easy to look at it, rather than around him at the corpses strewn about. In fact, it was more than easy to look at it, it was somehow comforting.

A stick of dynamite had Thaddeus Tremorlund entirely in its thrall. It somehow spoke to him. No; something other than words, it was providence. He had been staring at the very thing that could wipe away this blight on his perfect little life in an equally as perfect little town.

No thought of how the township could cope with a murderous monster. Nothing so magnanimous would ever enter his mind. All he could think of was that stick of dynamite burning away the problem that he was faced with. It was all so perfectly clear. All he had to do was blow up the evidence, and then there would be absolutely no proof that anything was wrong at all.

He was still clutching the small oil lamp in one hand. It was a minor miracle that he hadn't dropped it upon discovering the carnage in the mine. The dynamite was used to break up any granite deposits that may get in the way of the rich vein of Matlockite that the mine had presented. It wouldn't be enough to bring the walls or the ceiling of the cave down, but it would make a mess of the bodies. It would look exactly like the dynamite had killed the men. A dreadful accident.

He reached out and picked it up. It had an enormously long fuse on it. More than enough time for him to escape. He pondered the plan forming in his mind. He would light the fuse and escape. When he made it back to town he would say that he heard an explosion upon entering the mine and racing to the aide of the miners, he found all of them dead.

Thaddeus nodded. It all fitter together like a perfect puzzle. He could theorise that somebody dropped a lamp, just like the one he was holding now, onto the dynamite lighting the very end part of the fuse. The miners wouldn't have had a chance. It was a perfect solution. There would be nobody and nothing to say otherwise.

He was decisive. He uncoiled the fuse so that no parts of it were overlapping. He didn't want to minimise his escape time after all. Then positioning the dynamite in the middle of the bodies strewn around him, he walked away from the stick gently running the fuse between two of his fingers until he found the end. He touched his lamp to the end. It fizzled into life, spitting and hissing.

Thaddeus ran for his life. The journey through the mineshaft to the entrance was covered in record time. He didn't think that he had it in him. But the motivation of saving his own skin gave him the energy he needed to excel. Soon he was free of the rocky tunnel. He scampered for the nearest and largest tree that he could find. He settled himself behind it with fingers in his ears. It was an agonising wait, but his growing anticipation was rewarded with a calamitous explosion from deep within the mine.

Standing up he subconsciously wiped his hands together to dust them off. There was nothing more to do now than report this tragedy to the townsfolk.

Unseen by the Mayor a set of malevolent eyes watched him from a little further back into the surrounding forest. They followed his progress as he began his return journey to town. He had been secretly observed arriving. Entering the mine. But the creature did not make itself known to him. It was sated. It had feasted on the parts of the miners that pleased it. And yet, the nourishment had failed to provide the beast with exactly what it had wanted. One thing was for sure, the monster had plans for Mayor Thaddeus Tremorlund. All in good time. For now it was content to allow events to unfold as they were.

***

It was around six in the evening of quite a fateful day when the news broke in the town. All of the miners had been killed in an accident. A stick of dynamite had somehow become lit at the end of the fuse and detonated, killing all seven. The Mayor had found the bodies. He had heard the explosion upon his approach to the mine. He ran valiantly forward without thought of his own safety to do his best to help. But it was all to no avail. The Matlockite miners in Starkholmes had all died instantly.

Smedley had returned to work at the hydro centre when the news made it to him. Hurrying to the town hall he was unsurprised to see that a large contingent had gathered. The Mayor was in his usual position atop the external stairs. He appeared to be answering questions from the crowd. It was a cold evening; the sun had set, and the gas lanterns in the street were being lit. The encroachment of night would see the end to this Mayoral address soon enough. Smedley hurried forward to hear what was being said.

"Yes, yes absolutely tragic; all of those poor souls. And some of them married and leaving widows behind. It is a dark day in the history of our town. But we must be brave good people. I have declared tomorrow Saturday the fourth of March in the year of our Lord eighteen ninety-three to be a day of mourning for our loss. And thereafter, every year that marks this event, the third of March, to be a day of remembrance for those that we have lost."

The Mayor's words clearly found favour with the crowd who gave a resounding 'hear hear' in response. Someone was shouting a further question about the events, but it was waved away by the Mayor.

"Our thoughts must be with the two widows, they are being comforted as best as they can under these circumstances. As are the family members for all of those lost this day. I have sent for the parish Vicar and Priest. There was a mix of Church of England and Catholic amongst the dead. I have them in my office now and with your good permission, I wish to make the arrangements myself for the funerals for our honoured dead."

That seemed to bring an end to the impromptu town meeting. There was a general murmuring of approval for the generous deed that the Mayor now wished to undertake. He appeared to be discharged from his recounting of events by the crowd. Accordingly, he gave a small wave goodbye and turned to enter the town hall, presumably to meet the religious town leaders and make good on his promise to arrange the funerals.

Smedley couldn't help but feel that it was just too bizarre a coincidence. The very people that had been singled out by the ghostly apparition of Madam Alice Athalia had now been struck down by a dreadful accident.

He was still pondering this, when a hand touched his shoulder. He turned, it was Martha and Michael Morrell.

"You've heard?" he said dispensing with the usual pleasantries under the circumstances. Both Martha and Michael did not verbalise an answer. The grief on their faces and the small nods from the two of them were enough confirmation.

"I carry a heavy burden Mister Smedley."

Martha`s words were unexpected. Keith gave her a look of non-understanding.

"My Sister`s premonition. We assumed that it had something to do with the monster, but perhaps the two are not connected in this case. If only we had found a way to get to the miners sooner perhaps this tragedy could have been avoided."

"I don't think that you can blame yourself Missus Morrell. The Mayor took it upon himself to investigate the reference to the miners. Apparently, he was just too late."

The conversation between the two had garnered eves-droppers and more obvious attentions from some of the crowd nearest to them. A small group now crowded around the Morrells and Smedley.

"What's all this about Smedley? Do you know something about it all?"

Keith couldn't see who asked the question but felt obliged to answer.

"A séance held last night foretold of tragedy for the miners. I brought it to the attention of the Mayor and he felt that he should investigate himself."

The answer was as brief yet explanatory as Smedley was prepared to be at this point. It only cemented what the crowd had already surmised, that the Mayor was on a mission to the miners for reasons unknown. But now of course, the reason that he was in Starkholmes at the mine was evident. He held fears for the safety of the Matlockite miners.

"What a brave man" said a female voice from the crowd.

"Bless him, if only he were there in time to help them it may not have happened"

Another female voice from the crowd. But a third was not as complimentary.

"If only your séance had been held sooner this could have been prevented" the tone was accusatory. Martha and Michael looked uneasily at each other. Keith was now feeling a little nervous too. There was nothing like an angry mob and opinion could turn against someone in a heartbeat. He had to defuse the situation, lest they be branded as instigators of the unfortunate happening.

"Who's to say what *may* have happened. I think that the Mayor's announcement should be taken to heart, we have a day of mourning to prepare for tomorrow. It wouldn't surprise me that the funerals will be arranged quickly so that we reflect on the preciousness of life."

Smedley's words garnered a round of nods and 'ayes' from the crowd. Feeling that he had circumvented a backlash from the people he pointed out the obvious in the hope of ending this small inquisition.

"It's dark and cold and we have much to reflect upon; I think that it's best that we all go home"

It was a masterstroke. Indeed, it was cold, and a wind had started blowing making it particularly unpleasant to be loitering around the Town Hall. People acquiesced and began to move away.

"Should I see the two of you home?" Keith said loudly enough for people to hear. It was an obvious ploy, but one that worked. The crowd drifted away.

"What do you think?" Smedley asked when the others were out of earshot.

"It's hard to say. Does it have a connection to this horrible monster that is stalking the people of Matlock? Was it just a coincidence? I would need otherworldly guidance."

"Another séance?" asked Keith

"Another séance" confirmed Martha.

Chapter 14: The Second Séance

By the time the Morrells and Smedley had made it to Balmoral House it was close to 7pm. Martha had insisted that they dine first, saying that she couldn't bear the thought of holding a séance on an empty stomach. They ate, but Keith's appetite was almost non-existent after the events of the day.

***

The wind had picked up and was howling around the sharp stone corners of Balmoral House when Martha set up the main dining room for the séance. Candles were lit. Keith and Michael were seated at either side of the head of the table. The main gas lights in the dining room had been dimmed. The flickering candles gave rise to shadows dancing upon the walls.

Martha approached the table from lighting yet another candle on the mantlepiece. As she was taking her chair at the head of the table she told them a caveat that she felt they should know.

"Normally it would be a minimum of four people to hold a séance, or six or eight. Three is an odd number and not the best, but under the circumstances, I think that we should take the risk"

"Risk?" Keith was somewhat aghast that there was a risk to be taken by contacting the dearly departed.

“Brave heart Mister Smedley. What we are doing is for the sake of our community” Martha`s tone was unmistakably confident, yet she had not allayed Keith`s fears about what exactly constituted a *risk* by holding this séance.

There was a picture in a frame on the table. Keith indicated to it hoping to find out more about it.

“That is my sister, Madam Alice Athalia, Psychic to the crowned heads of Europe.” She explained, echoing the explanation that she had given Christian Mayweather not long ago.

Martha began her instruction. The clock in the dining room struck a single chime. Unconsciously they all looked at it. It was 8:30pm.

“Now, place both hands on the table before you, palms pressed to the tablecloth.”

They did as they were instructed.

“I am calling through the ether of the barrier from our world to the next. I am searching for my sister, Alice Athalia. Alice, if you can reach me, come through. We have need of your wisdom”

The words seemed to reverberate around the empty room. But somehow it did not feel empty anymore. The noise of the wind rose from a whine to a howl. Keith wasn’t too sure what to expect of the séance, but he had always thought that it would be lots of calling to the other-side and very little response. He was in for a complete shock.

A small girl appeared at the end of the table, perhaps two or three years old. She was glowing with an unearthly light. She said nothing, looking at them innocently.

“Welcome my dear, my name is Martha. Will you tell us who you are?”

Martha sounded for all the world like a teacher addressing a student.

The girl’s mouth opened, far too wide for a human mouth to stretch and a huge Boa-constrictor snake emerged and writhed, wrapping itself around the body of the girl.

Martha, Michael and Keith all tensed.

“Keep your hands pressed to the table! It is an evil spirit. If you lift your hands I cannot protect you!” Martha shouted her warning.

“Begone daemon! You are not welcome here!” The force of Martha’s rebuke was contrary to her small nature. The vision began to waver. The snake appeared to be crushing the girl. There was a sickly cracking of bones and the girls neck snapped like a dry twig. Her head pushed sideways in a grotesque angle.

“Begone! Back to the purgatory from which you came?” Martha yelled. And in an instant the snake and the little girl were gone.

“Oh, dear heavens!” said Smedley unable to keep his peace.

“Please Mister Smedley, I must have complete silence” begged Martha.

In spite of Keith's heart pounding loudly in his ears, he managed to compose himself enough to comply.

"Once more I call out to the spirits from beyond. Good spirits please help us, I seek to commune with my Sister Alice; Alice Athalia. Please Alice come to me now we are in dire need of your counsel.

Another figure appeared at the foot of the table. She was a woman in her late thirties by the look of her. Although well-dressed, she had a little too much make-up for polite society. She stared at Martha.

"You are welcome here if you are a good spirit. Speak, who are you?" demanded Martha.

"Elizabeth Stride" came the unthreatening response.

"Do you have a message for us Elizabeth? A message from my sister Alice?"

"Yes"

The response somehow eased the tensions in the room. This, for all of the unusual nature of the happening, was just a tarted-up woman that carried a message from beyond.

"What message to you have for us Elizabeth?" Marth asked.

Elizabeth did not answer verbally. She reached down as if about to put her hands into pockets that the dress clearly did not contain. Instead she pushed her hands into her lower abdomen and pulled out various innards of her gizzards. She offered them to the table, dripping with blood.

Keith could see now that the dress was torn. No not torn, cut and Elizabeth's dress was saturated in blood. The huge gash from which she had extracted her own vital organs was gaping before them.

Michael, Martha and Keith had to fight to maintain their composure. Martha's earlier words of keeping their hands upon the table to afford protection echoed in Keith's mind. He looked down at the table into which he was pressing the palms of his hands with fervour. It was easier to not look at the hideous apparition at the foot of the table.

"Begone; begone!" cried out Martha. When the three of them next dared to look up the disembowelled woman was gone.

Martha let out a huge sigh. Michael and Keith did not know if it was from relief or exasperation.

"I fear that I have contravened the rules for contacting the spirits from beyond the grave."

"What do you mean?" inquired Keith.

"The time is not right. I am not a proper medium as my sister was. I need to rely on the position of the moon and stars. There is as much astronomy and astrology in contacting the spirits as there is paranormal ability. And I fear that I need everything to be in perfect alignment in order to do this properly."

"Like it was for the first séance. It was a full moon" quipped in Michael.

“Indeed, it was my dear. And the constellations were in alignment. It was a perfect conjunction. But that has passed now. The next truly available opportunity to contact Alice may not be until the next full moon” concluded Martha.

“Easter Saturday” said Keith “April the first”

“That is when Michael’s nieces are visiting us from Manchester for Easter. Lift your palms from the table, I will call upon no more from the other side” assured Martha.

The séance was over, and so was any chance of contacting Alice Athalia to ask for guidance. They would not be in a position to do so until early next month. Who knows what could happen between now and then?

Suddenly the thought of walking home in the dark, in a howling gale sent a shiver through Smedley. He looked at Michael and Martha.

“Would it be alright…” he began.

“Of course, you may stay the night Mister Smedley. We wouldn’t think of having you travel the pathways of Matlock knowing that such danger lurks out there.”

Smedley was relieved. He would see if he could talk with the other business owners tomorrow and see what their thoughts were on the chain of events affecting their town. Until then, he felt somehow safe inside of the thick stone walls of Balmoral House.

Chapter 15: Saturday the 4th of March 1893

The night was a tempestuous one; there was wind, rain, sleet and some snow. But the morning arrived at last and it all seemed to fade away. Smedley had breakfasted with the Morrells and then after thanking them for their hospitality and agreeing with them, Martha mostly, that he would see if he could garner support for warning the town of the lurking danger from the other hydro owners, he left for town.

The morning although bright was misty. He followed the most efficient trail to town. Not quite thinking that it would have been the very pathway that Christian Mayweather had traversed only the morning before.

He passed the occasional rambler and dog walker but for the most part was alone on the roads and tracks that he travelled. It was really no surprise. As the town was observing a day of mourning, most people would have chosen a solemn and quite day of reflection at home. Socialising was simply not the proper thing to do under the circumstances.

He was pondering this and many other things when he became aware that he had entered a patch of mist so thick that he could not see more than a few feet in front of him. And he was clever enough to know that he was near the treacherous cliff that had claimed Christian Mayweather. He stopped and waited for the mist to thin out. It would be safer.

The moments dragged by and eventually a breeze began to move the veil onwards behind him. He could see the way ahead now it was still murky, but clear enough for him to continue. But the hairs on the back of his neck stood up. And he turned around. He could see the receding mist floating away from him. It was white and swirly and travelling as if it were walking the pathway itself.

The white shroud parted to reveal a frightening apparition. Keith didn't even have to wonder what it was; the way it moved, the form it took, it could only be the Monster. And it was heading directly toward him. Terror gripped him tighter than any vice; it was almost suffocating.

With an unplanned cry he ran away from it. His mind raced. Two men that he knew of had been killed by that thing. And more than likely the miners in Starkholmes too, if he could only prove it. But right now, the thing had its sights set firmly upon him.

Running through the trees pushing the stray branches away he felt at first total defeat. How could he survive this encounter when others had not? They too must have run for their lives, but it did them absolutely no good whatsoever.

No, if he was to get away from this creature, he would simply have to outsmart it somehow. He chanced a look behind him. The shapeless blob had grown legs and was in equal pursuit. Smedley ran faster, faster than he had ever run before. Another look behind him confirmed that the beast was matching his speed.

He only had seconds before it would be upon him. He only had seconds before he reached the cliff that had claimed the life of Christian Mayweather. A stray thought occurred to Smedley in his panic. What if Christian had not been thrown from the cliff by the monster, what if he had been so overwhelmed with fear that he threw himself off the cliff rather than fall into the merciless clutches of the creature?

And in that second Smedley knew exactly what to do. The cliff face was before him, the pathway curved around it in a gentle curve. Out of the corner of his eye he could see the thing move to overtake him and head him off.

Smedley ran forward with all of his bravery and might and hurled himself off the cliff twisting his body as he did. He could see the creature had grown arms and fists raising them in frustration at being denied its prize. It emitted a blood-curdling growl as it did so. Keith only had a second to take in the scene before gravity took hold and clutching him as surely as the monster would have it dragged him below the line of the cliff face.

The monster moved forward and leant out over the cliff, screaming in defeat and anger. The foliage was too thick for him to see the bottom of the cliff at this point. Again, it cried in anger and defeat. It had been denied it's prize. It shook its fists and stamped its legs. Arms and legs disappeared into the pulsating blob and it quivered in irritation.

Eventually, defeated it slithered away.

***

Keith Smedley's plan to save his own life had worked better than he had anticipated. As he fell he reached out clutching at the thick vines that he had identified in the hands of Christian Mayweather the day before. His legs too seemed to get caught up in the thickly growing pest. Before he knew it, his hands were full of vines, enough to slow his fall and his legs were tangled in vines preventing him from plummeting to the ground.

The vines stretched and held his weight like a bunch of elastic bands. But the weight and way that the vines were stretched had ruptured some and not others and Smedley's weight had pushed his entire body into the entanglement of hanging vines. It had effectively covered him from view. He could not see up though the leaves and vines. He could not see down either, so he could not tell how far he had fallen before saving himself.

But he could hear the creature bellowing in anger. He shuddered as the sound travelled through him. It sounded close. Or was it far up the cliff face? He couldn't tell. All he wanted was for it to go away. So, he waited.

Moments turned to minutes. Hanging onto the vines was easy. Some had wrapped themselves around his arms, others his legs, in fact as he took the time to look at his situation, he could see now that falling was now an impossibility.

The lack of the monster's cry was comforting. It must have surely gone by now? But now, he had to disentangle himself and climb down. Down to a level he could not see. He tried to push some of the vines away with his arms unsuccessfully. Then he tried with his legs and met with a little more success. Enough of a space was revealed that he could see the ground below. He was about twenty feet off the ground.

Another second and he would have impacted the ground below and most surely have died. Breathing a sigh of relief, he did his best to unwind the vines from his left arm. If he could just grab a few of them and lower himself down, he would be in the clear.

***

With a good deal of effort Smedley managed to lower himself gently to the ground. He checked himself and was amazed to find no broken bones at all. Looking up at the cliff face covered with the Orange Trumpet Vines he couldn't believe his luck. If he had given more thought to the plan to jump from the cliff and rely on the strong vines to capture him mid-fall he most certainly wouldn't have done it. But desperate times call for desperate measures. And in this case his gamble had paid off.

The creature *was* real. He had seen it. It had pursued him with intent to.....

He couldn't contemplate what it would have done to him had it been able to catch him. Right now, though, that did not matter. He had to tell the townsfolk that they were all in danger.

He looked around and thought of the best tracks and pathways that would lead him to the main road. Best not to take any chances here in the steep forest. The mists were still hovering here and there making him uneasy. Then deciding upon the route, he began his journey into town.

***

The day of mourning was not on Keith's mind as he approached the town hall. The town centre was bereft of it's usual Saturday markets. Although he could see the occasional shop had decided to open for business, they were for the most part closed. He walked resolutely up the outside steps of the Town Hall and entered the building. Striding down the hall he made is way directly to the office of the Mayor. Flinging open the door without bothering to knock he interrupted a rather large contingent filling up the room.

"What in heaven's name?" demanded the Mayor of the unannounced intrusion. The room had by happenstance all of the town seniors. The very people that Smedley had sought to speak with.

"I've seen it. It chased me through the forest pathways. Nearly got me!" he said almost babbling at all the men in the room.

"Seen what?" demanded the Mayor.

"The monster of course, it's hideous….." Smedley began but was immediately shouted down by the Mayor.

"Stuff and nonsense. I will not hear of this poppycock on our town`s day of mourning the tragic loss of so many of our own!" Thaddeus was clearly angry.

It was enough to stop Smedley in his tracks. Until now, he had forgotten about the day of mourning.

"But, it *is* real, I tell you, this *is* important. We are all in danger!" he retorted.

"For goodness sake Smedley. Have you no shame whatsoever!" shouted Tremorlund. This piqued Smedley's sense of honour. He felt insulted by the Mayor's accusation.

"This is not about honouring the recently departed *Thaddeus*! It is about saving the people of this town from a real and dangerous threat!" Smedley was annoyed and didn't mind showing it. He was going to make these people listen to reason, no matter how outlandish it seemed.

The scene had attracted others in the Town Hall and a small contingent began to form behind Smedley as he and the Mayor argued about the existence of the monster of Matlock. They continued to exchange verbal jousts neither one giving way from their point of view.

The other men in the office watched almost dumfounded at the vehemency at which the Mayor was trying to disparage Keith Smedley's story. The argument was going nowhere; so eventually William Aitkens of the Rockside hydropathic centre interceded.

"Thaddeus please! I know that it sounds outlandish, but I also know that Mister Smedley is not given to fanciful whim. There must be more to this than scare-mongering surely?"

The mayor glared at Aitkens and could be seen to draw a breath perhaps in preparation to launch a scathing verbal attack on Aitkens when Job Smith, also present spoke up. Given the amount of money that Job was pouring into the tramway and the town in general with his new hydropathic centre, the Mayor was not prepared to shout him down.

"Thaddeus, I agree with William. Please Keith recount your story for us from the beginning, without any interruptions please." Job gave the Mayor a look of warning.

So, Keith Smedley told them the story from the point of the previous night's séance and the visions it revealed. How he had stayed the night. Enjoyed breakfast with them this morning before setting out. The encounter with the creature and the daring way that he managed to elude it.

There was quite a crowd in the hall behind Smedley now. He only became aware of it when he stopped talking.

"And that was when I ran in here and tried to warn the Mayor that the monster is real."

His final sentence drew a reaction from the people. Keith turned to see that the hall was now full of people hanging on his every word. The story of the monster was sure to spread through the town now.

No matter how much the Mayor wanted to suppress the story, it would go from mouth to ear and mouth to ear, until the entire town and surrounding areas had heard it.

The thought occurred to Smedley that this is exactly what he wanted when he stormed into the Mayor's office. For the warning to be spread. Now, that was inevitable. Or so he thought. He looked at the Mayor expecting him to be seething with anger. Instead, Tremorlund was looking around at the people trying to gauge their reaction. He tapped his finger to his chin before approaching Smedley and asked a single question.

"What evidence do you have?"

"Evidence?" Smedley was taken aback. He thought for a moment and said

"You have my word as a gentleman"

"Oh! Is that a fact? And we are all supposed to take your word that this is not some cleverly concocted story by you, to win accolades for your bravado in eluding this thing that nobody other than yourself has seen. No doubt for the sole reason of nothing more than self-aggrandisement."

The accusation stung Smedley. He stammered in bewilderment.

"Self, self-aggrandisement. Me?"

“Yes, Mister Smedley. If not, then for what? said the Mayor with a snide tone.

“To warn the people of the danger of course!” he replied, defending his honour.

“I don’t believe you” Thaddeus was accusatory. A masterful public figure and politician, Thaddeus had planted a seed of doubt in the minds of all those listening. There were even a few people who supported the Mayor’s assertion with a ‘hear-hear’ in the background. Smedley couldn’t see who.

“We are all meant to take your story as if it were gospel from above without any evidence whatsoever, and without anybody else having seen this supposed, *monster*?” The Mayor’s tone had gone from accusing to mocking. A masterful stroke of deviousness from the seasoned town official. Thaddeus knew that all he had to do was plant the seed of doubt in the minds of all present. Popular opinion tended to err on the side of conservatism. And he intended to exploit that position.

And asking the townspeople to believe in something that they had not seen with their own eyes was perhaps asking for too much faith in one man. Smedley looked around, the people seemed divided. But not between those that believed and those that did not. It was more like those that wanted to be presented with hard evidence and those that simply discounted the story as fanciful.

“You believe me; don’t you?” Smedley asked of Job Smith and William Aitkens.

Both had furrowed brows. They did not answer immediately which was more than enough to damn Smedley to the ranks of self-promoting attention-grabber.

"Well Keith; it is perhaps something that would be best to have come from more than one person. I think that we have been very patient with you in this regard. But in light of nothing other than a message from beyond the grave, if you believe in that sort of thing, and an early morning pursuit by person or thing unknown……" Job Smith trailed off not wanting to complete his dissolution of the story that Smedley had asked them all to take upon faith alone.

Keith couldn't believe it. All he wanted to do was help the townsfolk. But now somehow the Mayor had turned the people against him. He looked around at the crowd for support. As expected, he found little to none. If there was, perhaps they were now simply reticent to say so in company.

Smedley was embarrassed and angry. He shook his head in exasperation.

"What will it take to convince you? Another death! That is most surely how Christian Mayweather and Albert Brawnly died" he said.

"Know that for a fact do you?" challenged Thaddeus.

"That is not what the *official* report said. Death by falling from a great height. Not a sign of monster marks on them anywhere!" Thaddeus wriggled his fingers and thumbs in an orchestrated mocking way. Some people laughed at the comical nature of it.

Smedley knew that he was all but defeated. He looked around for support but found none. Not even from his fellow business owners and people that he considered friends. There was nothing to it, he either had to come up with hard evidence to support his claim, or he had to retract his story in the hope of saving some face. But neither prospect seemed appealing right now.

Crestfallen he turned around to leave. The people behind him parted allowing him easy exit. Without a further word, Keith Smedley left the Town Hall and made his way in the direction of Smedley's Hydro. There at least, he could find some solace. Time to think. Time to ponder everything that had transpired.

Chapter 16: Nightfall

Keith had sat in his office at Smedley's Hydro since returning from his humiliation at the Town Hall. His staff had brought him a sandwich for lunch which sat uneaten on a plate he had pushed to the side of his large polished oak desk. Minor administrative duties had distracted him throughout the day, but as the evening came, there was less to occupy him, and his mind began to play through the scene from the morning. He was depressed.

The abject silence brought his pondering to an end. He looked up thorough the clear glass panels that separated his office from one of the main hydro pools. It was empty. He looked at the clock. It was 7pm.

All of the guests would be at dinner by now. And the staff too, taking the opportunity to dine in the staff allocated dining room. He was alone.

He was being watched. Inhuman eyes, or an approximation of eyes regarded Keith Smedley. Beneath the water in the main hydro pool it was lurking.

Keith got up from his desk and stretched and yawned. He was sore from being immobile for so long. He opened the door and stepped out into the main pool room. His footsteps echoing in the voluminous space. Unknowingly he was walking right toward the creature.

Keith stepped to the edge of the main pool and squatted down to feel the water. It was just the right temperature. He could feel the minerality in the water. He let his hand drip for a few moments when he took it out before shaking it and wiping it on his dark trousers. He stood up and then noticed something in the water.

It was difficult to see, as if it were transparent in places but not others. Was it his imagination or was there something there? And was it moving closer to him or was that too just his eyesight playing tricks on him? He peered trying desperately to focus upon something that he could barely see.

Then it erupted from the water with flailing tentacles and misshapen body. Keith jumped backwards. The thing was huge, at least the same size as him. It landed with a splash on the tiled floor barely a foot from him. Panicked Keith ran the length of the pool toward the door that led to the smaller mineral baths. He daren't look behind him for fear of seeing how close the beast was that was chasing him. He could perceive that it was in pursuit. He thought.

Flinging open the doors he almost collected two patrons that where donning their robes having emerged from the heated mineral pools. Two older gentlemen. He looked in terror at them and turned around to ascertain where the creature was that was pursuing him. There was nothing there. The main pool room was empty.

"What on earth are you doing Mister Smedley?" asked one of the men clearly horrified at the sudden intrusion.

Keith looked at him and then back into the empty main pool room again as if trying to convince himself that he had indeed seen something, and it had actually chased him. Hadn't it?

"Well, spit it out man. What is it? What's the matter?"

Keith's mind raced. He did not want a repeat of this morning's debacle. There was no monster behind him. There was nowhere it could have possibly gone except maybe in the main pool again.

"Ahh" he said.

"I thought that I heard a cry for help?" he said as convincingly as possible.

"No, not from me. What about you Smithley?" one old man asked his companion.

"Not me. I didn't hear anything" they both regarded Smedley.

"Oh, I am sorry. I didn't mean to alarm you gentlemen. How are you enjoying your stay here at Semdley's?" he said trying to recover the awkward situation.

Faced with something that they did know all about, both managed an ebullient critique of the facilities and their rooms and the staff. All the while Keith kept looking back into the main pool room door, holding it open so that he could see the room in its entirety. There was nothing out of place.

"Thank you very much for your kind words gentleman. Can I see you to your rooms?" he inquired.

"Very kind, but no thank you. We are late for dinner. A quick change and then see you in the dining room at our usual table, eh?" one said to the other. It was agreed. They picked up their belongings and started to exit, just as an unexpected hand came down upon Keith's shoulder from behind.

With a loud cry of alarm Smedley spun around to see what had accosted him. It was Mister Griffin, a long-time repeat customer of the establishment.

"Steady on Mister Smedley" said Mister Griffin. "It's only me"

"You came from the main pool room?" asked Keith with a note of alarm.

"Yes, from the steam room at the end; why?" he asked, puzzled at the interrogation. But then he noticed the two other patrons and bid them a good evening. They left, and Keith was alone with Mister Griffin.

"I wanted to talk to you about the.....story that you told this morning at the Town Hall" said Griffin.

"Were you there?" inquired Smedley

"No, but I heard a first-hand account of what you said from a friend who was. There are the believers amongst the townsfolk. Two mysterious deaths so close to each other. I don't know what to make of the mining tragedy. But people are unsettled. And I wonder if it is wise to bring forth a story about a monster lurking in the dark somewhere watching and waiting to strike. But at the same time, it would explain quite a lot. People can be swayed so easily in times like these. Do you see what I am saying?" The middle-aged gentleman waited for Smedley's reply.

But Keith did not understand the point of what had been said. From his point of view, it looked like he was both being supported and admonished in equal measure.

"Uh; no"

"Come with me to see about that steam room vent. We'll talk some more" offered Griffin.

"Vent?" Smedley was puzzled.

"Oh; didn't I say? That's why I wanted to speak with you. One of the main steam room vents appears to be clogged; or not emitting enough steam for some reason. I was hoping that you could take a look at it?" Griffin said.

Faced with a normal administrative duty, Smedley relaxed visibly.

"Yes of course, please after you Mister Griffin" Smedley indicated that the guest should proceed him back into the main swimming pool room.

They walked the length of the exceptionally long pool chatting about the events of the recent past. All the while Smedley was watching the pool for any sign of the creature.

Something irked Keith as they made their way to the steam room at the end of the swimming pool. Mister Griffin did not appear to be wearing clothing that would have been appropriate for taking a steam room session. And he did appear out of the area that the monster was last seen. And, according to Martha

Morrell, via Alice Athalia, the beast could assume a human form.

Keith's eyes narrowed as he regarded Griffin. An uneasiness came over him. He was alone at the far side of the sizeable hydropathic establishment. A cry for help from here would go unheard in the dining room separated by multiple thick stone walls.

"Here it is, the main vent at the far side of the room, bottom one, beneath the wooden bench seat." Griffin's instructions were precise. Smedley opened the door the square room was unsurprisingly filled with steam. He looked at Griffin who had a po-faced expression.

Something wasn't right, and Smedley knew it.

"I'll have our handyman look at it first thing after dinner" offered Smedley.

"It may be nothing, you're here now; take a look" Griffin's tone was firm.

It would appear odd at this point to not investigate. But Keith was torn. If this was the beast it could attack him now; why wait till he was in the steam room? There was no help for him. He felt like a chicken that had unwittingly wandered into a fox's den.

Without any valid reason to object he entered the room. Steam filled his nostrils. The scent of lavender that was mixed with the steam enveloped him.

"Straight ahead of you" instructed Griffin

Smedley crossed the room. The thickness of the steam made it difficult to see. The lighting was diffused by the steam, making everything emanate with an eerie glow. An impending sense of dread began to crush Keith. He looked around at Griffin. He was holding open the door. He had not moved.

Keith bent down to inspect the steam outlet point. It appeared to be emitting a normal amount of steam to him. Behind him he heard the door close. Smedley looked around, Griffin had entered the room and allowed the door to close behind him.

"It looks alright to me" said Keith, hoping that he managed to keep the nerves out of his voice. Griffin didn't say a word but approached, slowly and deliberately. Keith stood up. Griffin was barely five feet away from him. Griffin's eyes seemed glazed as they held Smedley's gaze.

Smedley's mind raced. If he could somehow distract Griffin, he could dart around him and perhaps make it to the door. As if in anticipation of the initiative, Griffin spread out his arms effectively cutting off any hope of escape for Keith. Smedley's heart pounded loudly in his chest and in his ears. There was nowhere for Keith to go, he couldn't get away from this situation.

Griffin approached and at the point where panic was about to take over Smedley and he was about to push Griffin out of the way with all his might and run for his life, the door to the steam room opened. They both looked up.

Standing at the door was a familiar silhouette. Its identity given by the lilting voice that spoke.

"Gentleman, you're not really dressed for a steam room therapy session?" The voice was of Mary Whittaker, owner of the Matlock Bath Mineral Water Works.

Smedley breathed a sigh of relief. He looked at Griffin, it was impossible to tell anything from his features. But he did speak.

"It must have righted itself somehow. Sorry to bother you Mister Smedley. It's about time I went to dinner. Good evening to you both"

With the pleasantries over he excused himself and left. Mary Stood aside to allow him egress. Smedley following closely behind. He breathed another sigh.

"It's good to see you Mary" he said with genuine relief.

"I couldn't find you in your office and noticed the steam at the far end of the main pool room, so I surmised that you may have been in here. Simple detective work Keith. Now, let's get on with our negotiations for next years supply of mineral waters to your burgeoning establishment, shall we?"

The reason that Mary Whittaker was there now dawned on Smedley. This meeting was arranged weeks ago. Mary wanted to negotiate a new deal for the supply of mineral waters from Matlock Bath to Smedley's hydro. The current contract coming to a natural conclusion toward the middle of the year. Her reference to the centre being burgeoning clearly indicative of a want for a better price for her product.

“Yes of course, let’s convene our talks in my office, shall we?” he indicated that they should make their way across the room to his usual place of business.

Smiling confidently, perhaps because she was confident of obtaining a better deal in her favour, she nodded in agreement and led the way.

Smedley tried his best to cover up the fact that he felt that he had just been saved from certain molestation by a creature hiding in the form of one of his guests. But it wouldn’t do to talk of such things. He was already basically labelled a story-teller without offering proof. Something just short of being accused as a liar. He did not want to descend into being suspected of being mentally unbalanced.

***

Mary had been a tough negotiator, but it was done. They had both agreed on a new price for the supply of mineral waters from Mary’s establishment to Smedley’s Hydro. They were toasting the new deal with a fine Baron Otard cognac that Keith kept in his office. Mary clearly had something other than the new contract arrangement on her mind.

“Keith; may I be direct?” she asked. He could tell from her voice that it was something other than business that she had on her mind.

“Of course, Mary; please do” he replied

“I don’t want to see a high-profile businessman such as yourself, brought down in the eyes of the people of Matlock. You know to what I am referring?” it was a rhetorical question. She continued.

“I won’t say one way or the other if I believe the account of events that you and Martha and Michael Morrell have come to represent. But I will say this; if there is something untoward going on in Matlock, then it is better for everyone that we know.” The sentiment was completely neutral. Smedley agreed with her.

“So, then, if you can investigate the goings on in a more surreptitious manner then it would be better for your reputation, and in the best interests of everyone. Don’t you agree?’ Mary was clearly hedging her bets in this instance. She was neither committing to believing the monster story, nor dismissing it as imaginative fantasy.

She must make a terrific poker player, thought Smedley. It was impossible to tell what her real point of view was. But she was encouraging him to proceed cautiously and come up with some hard evidence to support his belief.

“I understand your meaning Mary, and I think that it is the best course of action at this point in time” he said, agreeing with her.

Mary looked relieved and smiled whilst taking another sip of the fine cognac.

“I’m glad” she said.

“Promise me one thing though Mary?” Keith pleaded.

"What is it?"

"If anything happens to me, then you can rest assured that it has something to do with the creature. It knows that I know about it, and I believe that it will target me as its next victim. As surely as you are sitting in a chair before me, I *know* that this insidious thing wants to do me harm."

The resolute tone and absolutism of the statement struck Mary. She looked like she was about to argue the point, but instead acceded.

"Very well; I shall. Should anything happen to you, I will take up the mantle and insist that the authorities take the matter very seriously. You have my word"

Even her acquiescence was duplicitous. Somehow reassured but not quite, Keith lifted his glass to toast to Mary's avowal.

After they had finished their drinks and Mary had left, Keith saw signs of life returning to the main swimming pool area. Patrons were getting in their last mineral water swims before retiring for the night.

He sat in his office contemplating his next move. Keith knew that there would be no more consorting with the spirit-world until the moon was again full. So, he would have to rely upon the living to aide and abet his investigations. But were to start?

Chapter 17: The Following Week

The funeral service and funeral mass for the miners were arranged for Friday the 10th of march. At disparate times, the Mayor was able to speak at both. He gave a rousing speech of praise for the men who helped put Matlock on the map by putting Matlockite into every school and university and other science institution around the world. But that. although tinged with loss right now, the future was brighter for Matlock. The celebrations for the opening of the cable car tram would go on nevertheless.

It was a way to bring together the people and look to the future of Matlock. It was announced that the new cable car tram would be written-up in the next printed edition of Bradshaw's Guide to Britain. The definitive tourist guide to the length and breadth of the British Isles. It would further consolidate Matlock as a destination for people from all over the kingdom. The Mayor had confirmed the inclusion with the author himself via the publisher.

The Mayor's combined eulogy and statement of praise for the future of the town met with approval from everyone. He didn't mention or even hint at the undertone of the monster story pervading people's casual conversation. A week had gone by without any sign of it, and the people were beginning to lose interest in something that could not be substantiated. The

Mayor was not going to give it any more credence by acknowledging it at all.

Martha, Michael, Elizabeth and Keith were at the grave for the lowering of the coffins into the ground. They conversed about how to come up with hard evidence to support what they knew. But it soon became obvious that they were earning the ire of the townsfolk. So, any further conversation about the monster in a public place was quashed.

***

It was a glorious day. Monday the 13th of March. The cold weather seemed to have disappeared, temporarily at least. The sky was a brilliant shade of blue and there was barely a cloud to be seen. Mayor Thaddeus Tremorlund and his wife were with Job Smith and his entourage. They were at the highest part of the town. It had been decided that as part of the celebrations for the opening of the cable tram car, on schedule to happen on the 28th of the month, that hot air balloon rides would be available for those adventurous enough to undertake one.

The balloon gondola housing the operator, introduced by Job Smith to the Mayor and Tiffany Tremorlund simply as Ben, would be accompanied by two people at a time. The balloon was tethered to a rope on a large spool that wound itself out as the balloon would rise, and two sturdy men could then winch it back down to the same place from which it took off.

"Ready for a trial run Thaddeus, Tiffany?" Job inquired of the couple.

"How exciting. I only hope that I don't scream, or feint" Tiffany could barely contain her enthusiasm.

Steps were ready to assist the couple into the gondola. Thaddeus helped his wife up the steps and Ben lifted her into the basket. The Mayor made a not-so-elegant entry into the gondola but righted himself with as much dignity as he could muster. Nobody seemed to notice or care.

"Ready?" asked Ben, the balloon operator.

"Oh yes, indeed we are" affirmed Tiffany.

Ben did something to the mechanism and a plume of fire erupted from the top of it. Nothing happened immediately but with another two purges of fire into the hovering balloon above them they began to lift off from the ground.

The small contingent cheered. Thaddeus and Tiffany gave regal waves to the onlookers as they rose higher and higher. It was an elegant way to travel, thought the Mayor. Floating gently upwards, this must be how butterflies see the world. It wasn't long before the majesty of the surrounding town and countryside took over the attentions of the couple.

"Look dear you can see all the way to the Castle" Tiffany pointed with her gloved hand. And it was true, the castle in Riber a hamlet next to Matlock could be clearly seen. It's imposing gothic architecture on display from an angle that only birds would have seen before.

There was a sudden jerk on the line holding the balloon to the ground.

"What is it, what's wrong?" asked the Mayor a little nervously.

"Nothing at all Mayor Tremourlund. We've reached the end of the rope. They will leave us here for a few minutes and then begin to winch us down. So, I can turn this off then. I won't be needing it until another ascent." Ben indicated to the flame mechanism that had been responsible for their flight.

"We are just far enough from the ground that people may hear you scream, but they won't be able to make out anything that you shout down to them"

Ben's rather curious fact garnered looks of vexation from both Thaddeus and Tiffany.

"You don't say?" said the Mayor, unsure of how to respond to the odd fact. For his part Ben smiled at the both of them in a rather unsettling way.

"I wasn't properly introduced by Job Smith, so please allow me to do the honour. My name is Captain Benjamin Brigges of the merchant brigantine Mary Celeste."

The reference was completely lost on both Thaddeus and Tiffany who looked at each other with a mixture of bemusement and worry. But those petty emotions were soon to be overtaken by horror as they watched Ben's face began to dissolve. Only his mouth was left. Chillingly it spoke further.

"But I have come to be known as the Monster of Matlock"

Tiffany screamed at the top of her lungs. Thaddeus looked over the edge and actually contemplated scurrying down the rope tethering them to the ground. There was nowhere to go. The creature was in the basket with them. They were surely doomed. They would be killed in front of everyone but without anyone able to help them.

Benjamin's face returned to normal and he laughed at their distress. He seemed to revel in the torture that he was causing the couple. They were completely powerless and in his grip.

"Oh Thaddeus, you of all the people in Matlock have nothing to fear from me. I've come to think of you as a friend. No! An accomplice in the recent happenings in this lovely little town." Benjamin's words were so completely unexpected that all Thaddeus could do was gulp and shake his head.

"Surely you have thought of us as partners Thaddeus. I have killed, you have covered it up. Those poor miners. But such an imaginative solution to hide my carnage." Ben held the Mayor's gaze steadily.

Tiffany managed to get her heart out of her throat for long enough to challenge what had been said.

"Thaddeus what is this, this, thing saying? Do you know this creature?"

"No; no!" he said, feebly attempting to defend himself.

"Oh, my dear Tiffany. Your charming husband came across the bodies of the miners that I had ripped apart and eaten. But decided that rather than admit that a monster was lurking in the countryside surrounding Matlock, that dynamite would effectively cover up the entire incident. And you were absolutely correct Thaddeus. It was a brilliant stroke of ingenuity. I congratulate you" Benjamin seemed genuinely pleased with Thaddeus. The very human emotion took out some of the fear from the encounter. Thaddeus was blushing, his sin had been revealed to his wife.

"Thaddeus; no!?" was all that Tiffany could say.

"But that is not all. Didn't he tell you about my first encounter with a villager. What was his name? Albert, something?" Benjamin stroked his beard trying to remember the name of the first victim of the Monster of Matlock.

"Brawnly" said Tiffany.

"That's it. Albert Brawnly. Who saw me as plainly as we see each other now. And tried to raise the alarm. But Thaddeus managed to get the poor man so intoxicated that it was easy lead him to the dangerous part of the cliff top walking path and push him off. Better that than have the story of a monster tarnish your perfect little town, eh Thaddeus?" Benjamin laid bare Thaddeus's other mortal sin. The murder of Albert Brawnly.

Thaddeus could barely look up at his wife. He was a murderer and he thought that he had got away with it so perfectly, until now. It was a while before he could bring himself to speak.

"And now your going to kill me; us?" he said dejectedly.

"Of course not, why ever would I do anything so abhorrent?" the irony of the statement was lost on both

Thaddeus and Tiffany. All they took from the statement was that they were not about to be murdered.

“I don’t understand” said Thaddeus.

“I think that we can work together. I can go on living here amongst you. Feeding on the occasional traveller maybe. But I will need someone to help cover up any of my indiscretions. Occasionally I may lose my self-control and run amok. As I did in the mine. In those instances, it would be best if there was an official ready to take over and shall we say gloss-over the details, if you know what I mean? And that man is you Thaddeus.”

Mayor Tremorlund couldn’t believe what he was hearing. He was being recruited to be an accomplice to this creature.

“What makes you think that I will help you?” he said rather stupidly, not thinking before he spoke.

“But you already have Thaddeus. That is why I have arranged to meet you like this and secure your help. And right now, I need help with a particularly troublesome person by the name of Keith Smedley. He has managed to elude me twice now. I don’t intend that he should escape me a third time.”

The words stung Thaddeus. He had gone out of his way to discredit Smedley and the Morrells rantings about a monster secretly terrorising the town. But of course, it was all true. Thaddeus was in so deep now there was no turning back. Nevertheless, it felt like he was making a deal with the devil himself. He didn’t know what to say.

“And I could of course make it worth your while to aid and abet me” Benjamin pulled three rings from his waistcoat pocket. They had the biggest diamonds on them that Tiffany or Thaddeus had ever seen.

“From the French jewellery Maison of Chaumet. I acquired them during my Captaincy of the Mary Celeste.”

Instantaneous lust gripped Tiffany more completely than the fear that had enveloped her. The sparkling diamonds were the most brilliant that she had ever seen in her life. Benjamin could see the desire in her eyes. He handed the three of them to her.

“Dear, heavens, I have never-before seen the like” she said. Now, not even thinking that a monster in human form had handed the objects of desire to her.

Benjamin indicated that she should return them.

“All in good time. First, we have to do something about that troublesome Mister Keith Smedley.” He took possession of the rings from the Mayor’s wife. As he repocketed them her eyes followed them the entire time.

Tiffany gripped Thaddeus’s arm.

“We are reasonable people Mister…..I am sorry, *Captain* Brigges. I am sure that we can come to a suitable arrangement. Can’t we my dear?” her tone was uncharacteristically firm with Thaddeus. He looked at her. She had basically swept away the fact that he had murdered Albert Brawnly and covered up the deaths of the miners all within minutes of discovering his crimes.

“Uh, yes; yes, of course” he managed to stammer.

“Excellent” smiled Brigges. Benjamin had read the personalities of his accomplices well. He had them exactly where he wanted them.

At that moment the rope could be felt to begin winching them back toward the safety of the ground.

“You can profit from our little bargain Thaddeus. And the township of Matlock need never know that a *monster* hides amongst them, or rather *two monsters*. It really will be the perfect arrangement.”

Strangely, the words were comforting. It harkened to something normal that Thaddeus could deal with. This was a bargain pure and simple. It may be with a creature that kills and eats people. But it was a reciprocal deal nonetheless. And more importantly, his wife was now involved. She could share the burden. It felt wrong, but he was relieved. The reference by Benjamin, calling Thaddeus the second Monster of Matlock was not lost on him, but it was something that he could in no way deny.

The journey down to the ground seemed to take forever. The two burley men below could be seen winching the rope in with all their might. But soon they were greeted by an enthusiastic crowd as the gondola touched solid ground. People waved and cheered as they touched ground. Steps were put in place and Tiffany helped out of the basket first followed by Thaddeus.

"How was that?" asked Job Smith beaming from ear to ear.

The mayor couldn't help himself, he smiled broadly. But, it was just the fact that he was glad to be alive, however it would be mistaken by the onlookers as happiness derived from the airborne experience.

"I think that I can say without hesitation Mister Smith, that that was the most extraordinary experience that I have ever had in my life. Wouldn't you agree my dear?" He looked to his wife for affirmation. Her reply was masterful double-entendre.

"A shining experience Thaddeus. In fact, one could say without a shadow of doubt that, it was absolutely brilliant!"

Chapter 18: Tuesday the 14th of March 1893

Smedley had met with the Morrells at Balmoral House, but they could not find a way forward. They needed hard evidence to support what they knew. But there was simply none to be had. It was decided that the next séance to be held on the full moon Saturday the 1st of April would focus upon having the spirit world point them toward the evidence that they needed to convince the townsfolk of the danger that they were facing.

The daily routine of running one of the larger hydro establishments in the area had overtaken Keith Smedley. He had settled back into his comfortable little life when something happened.

He returned from lunching with some of the big-spending regular patrons and there was a note on his desk. It was in an envelope addressed to him. The hand writing was ornate yet still quite generic. It could belong to anyone. The envelope was of good quality, but nothing ostentatious. It may have been purchased at the post office or the local market. It was impossible to tell.

Keith opened the letter and studied the contents. It was dated today.

I am taking a risk by writing to you Mister Smedley. I feel that I am being watched by the very thing that you have spoken of, and tried in vain, to warn the town about.

I too have had an encounter with the creature. For that is what it is, a beast of some description that defies classification or reason. Furtive and irresistible, it is capable of hiding amongst us without being detected.

Yet I may hold the one thing that could prove, scientifically, the existence of the monster of Matlock. A specimen from the animal, if that is what it is? A piece of itself that I struck off with a knife in an attempt to defend myself during an attack.

If you could take this specimen to a scientific institute and have it positively identified, then it may hold the key to uncovering the beast and its nefarious doings.

You must forgive me my cowardice in this matter mister Smedley. I fear for my own life and do not wish to tempt fate by becoming more involved that I already am.

I have arranged a story to ensure that nobody notices my absence tomorrow, Wednesday night at half past eight. You will see when we meet that anonymity is paramount for me, as I am a public figure of good standing.

Please meet me them in the Wesleyan Chapel that is half way up Bank Road so that I may present you with the evidence of the monster.

Yours in hope and faith

A friend

Keith could hardly believe his eyes. This was exactly what he needed. Just seeing the words written down that there was somebody else that had encountered the monster was gratifying. His mind raced. A piece of the creature. It couldn't be anymore perfect. That would be more than enough evidence, if properly identified, to support the fact that the town was harbouring a sly and despicable creature.

He read the note from beginning to end again. The way that it was signed-off, although anonymous, led Smedley to believe that it may be a clergyman of some description. The assumption supported by the odd choice of meeting place. Where else would a man of the cloth feel safer?

He read the note a third time to ensure that he was not missing any necessary detail. He was not. But the further reading gave Smedley more sense that this was a town figure that was involved in religion in some way. He mused that the very existence of this beast may conflict with the beliefs that the man held. Perhaps that is why he did not want to be involved with the unmasking of the thing? But he could stand there and speculate all day. What mattered now is that he had an absolute believer to meet with tomorrow night.

He folded the note and was about to place it in his pocket when he thought the better of it. He unfurled it and laid it on the leather writing mat on his desk. Placing a paperweight on the corner. He looked at it for a short while when a staff member interrupted him.

"Mister Smedley. One of the valves that regulates the mineral water supply from the Matlock Bath Water Works has become stuck in the off position. We need to replenish the waters in the individual baths at the side of the establishment."

It was a problem that Keith had encountered before. He looked at the staff member. It was one of the newer young men that had come on-board. He would be unfamiliar with the nuances of that particular valve.

"I know the problem. I'll come and show you how to deal with the valve. It is rather temperamental, but if you know how to handle it, there is a way to coax it into submission".

He smiled and waved the young man on to lead the way. They left the office. There was a crowd of women all in immaculate bathing robes just at the close edge of the main swimming pool near the door to Smedley's office. One of them turned around.

"Was that Mister Smedley that just left?" she asked of her troupe.

"Yes, Tiffany, I believe that it was. Why?" asked one of Tiffany Tremorlund`s friends.

"Oh, I wanted a word. There is no telling when he will return? I know, I shall leave a note on his desk." She declared and brazenly marched into the office. The group of friends that Tiffany was with took only the slightest of notice before they went back to gossiping about the goings on in their circle of friends.

It was too perfect. Tiffany saw the note that she had authored with help from Thaddeus. It, along with the envelope that had contained it were spread out on the large desk, held down with a paper-weight.

The small fire in the office was flickering with more than enough life to engulf the incriminating letter. She picked up the pieces of paper and after ensuring that nobody was watching crumpled them up and threw them into the fire. They caught alight immediately and were consumed.

Sure, that the note was now nothing more than burnt ashes, unrecognizable, Tiffany left the office to re-join her friends. Phase one of their trap was set. She and Thaddeus and their newfound accomplice, Benjamin only needed to spring the trap and the troublesome Mister Keith Smedley would meet with an unfortunate and tragic accident.

Tiffany looked at her hands. She wondered which one she would wear the Chaumet rings upon. Perhaps both? She could see them now, beautiful, big, perfect diamonds. Her friends would be satisfyingly jealous. She had already come up with a story about them being left to her by an ancient aunt that suddenly passed away. It was all coming together with amazing ease.

Chapter 19: Wednesday 15th March 1893

The fact that the note had gone missing from Smedley's office was disturbing enough. But now that the night for the clandestine meeting had come, he was on edge because of the relentless weather. It had rained all day. It felt oppressing and foreboding. Mercifully it had stopped raining when he left the hydro to rendezvous with his informant.

He had managed to let the Morrells know about the meeting. They had insisted on accompanying him, but Keith talked them out of it. They were elderly, and he feared for the reaction of the note's author should he show up with them in tow. He promised to let them know the outcome of the meeting.

***

Bank road was steep. Lucky for him that Smedley's hydro was at the top of the hill and the journey down to the Chapel was easy for him. The gas lanterns were lit. But the damp had kept people in their homes. Nevertheless, the main road was still a little lively. The engineers were testing the cable tram car. It ran from Crown Square at the bottom of Bank Road all the way up past the Smedley and Rockside Hydro establishments, to the final part of Bank Road, which became Rutland Street. And nicely depositing the paying passengers practically at the doorstep to Job Smith's new hydro establishment, still under construction.

He was passing a small clique of men observing the intricacies of yet another test run of the car when a woman came out of her house to challenge the men. She was clearly annoyed and let the men working on the cable car know it.

"When will you be finished with that noisy thing? It never stops. Goes at all hours of day and night it does." She addressed all the men there unsure of who was in charge.

The project manager made himself known to her by answering.

"Just some last-minute teething problems that we will have sorted out long before the official opening on the twenty-eight of this month madam"

His response was tactful, but non-committal as to when they were planning to give up their night-time work.

Smedley scratched the back of his neck. It appeared that not everybody was as enthusiastic about Job Smith's cable tram car as he would have thought. It certainly would help deliver more people from the Matlock train station at the bottom of the hill to his establishment. So, he of course, was a huge supporter of the project.

The woman threw up her arms in exasperation making a suitable noise and stomped off back to her home closing the front door loudly.

"Maybe we'd better give it up for the night" he could hear the project manager saying to his men.

“Good evening” said Smedley as he passed, giving the men a wave, which was returned in kind.

There were a few spots of rain that touched Keith’s face. If that didn’t convince the men to give up working on the cable car for the night, then nothing would. He continued upon his way. Soon they were quite a distance behind him. At this point of the system, the tram tracks split into two. A masterful use of materials saw that the track was only done as a single line for the top and bottom part of the road, but here in the middle, where the tram cars would pass each other, was doubled up. This would allow the ascending car to pass the descending one. Then as each reached the climax or trough of its journey there was a semi-circular turning section of track. Thus, the cable tram car would always be operating in a clockwise direction.

Keith knew that it was based upon the cable cars of San Francisco that Job Smith had been so taken with upon a holiday there years ago. When he had decided with his great wealth to open a third large-scale hydro establishment in Matlock he saw the opportunity to donate a cable car to the township. One that would assure easy passage from the station to his business at the highest point of the town. Thankfully he was generous enough to allow others to benefit from his philanthropy.

It was getting colder. A sure sign that more rain was on the way. He could see the Wesleyan Chapel further down the street. It had a light inside. Not unusual for a local chapel. He strained to think of the pastor’s name that was in residence in the small cottage to the side. He wondered if that was the man that had written him the note about the surreptitious meeting? Soon all would be revealed he thought.

He approached the heavy wooden double doors. They were typically shaped in a gothic style. He lifted the latch and opened on side of the door. It creaked open ominously.

There was a small entry vestibule that led to the main part of the chapel. The wooden pews could be seen sitting idly row after row. Candles were lit here and there. The main source of light was a gas lantern suspended from above the small alter. There was movement. Smedley could see the back of somebody reaching over the alter to light a further candle. The scene looked so ordinary for the surroundings that it took the edge off Smedley's nervousness.

He shut the door behind him and entered the main part of the Chapel. The person at the alter had clearly heard the entry but did not turn around. Instead he indicated with a wave of his hand that Keith should join him at the front of the Chapel. Keith's shoes echoed on the stone floor.

He came to within ten feet of the man and stopped. The man turned around. Keith did not recognise him at all. They looked at each other without talking. The man was in his thirties maybe. With a beard and a hat that would look more at home on the sea than in a country town in the middle of Derbyshire.

"Who are you?" asked Keith unable to contain his curiosity any longer.

“Captain Benjamin Brigges of the merchant Brigantine Mary Celeste; at your service my good sir”

The greeting was so completely normal that it left Smedley with no immediate follow up. He had not heard of the ship in question. Should he asked for more details or inquire as to why a merchant ship’s Captain was here in Matlock? Instead he asked the obvious.

“You left the note for me?”

“Ah yes, the Monster of Matlock. It has quite a ring to it don’t you think?” Brigges answer did nothing to clarify the situation. Brigges attitude did not bely that he was particularly upset that a monster was lurking in the town or surrounding forest somewhere.

“You have something for me?” Keith was insistent that they get down to business.

“I do indeed Mister Smedley’ I do indeed” Brigges smiled malevolently. Keith’s blood began to turn cold.

As he regarded Brigges face with a growing concern he noticed that it was emanating a green glow that appeared to be coming from beneath the skin. Smedley took an involuntary step backwards. Brigges face dissolved and reformed into another. It was the most extraordinary thing that Smedley had ever seen.

“What is this?” Keith was torn. He was panicked yet desperate to know more.

“Junior Detective Inspector Samuel Gates; of the criminal investigation department, Metropolitan Police Force, London; reporting for duty sir!”

The person was completely different. The voice too. This was a younger man, blonde hair not dark. No beard and with piercing blue eyes.

It was all clear to Keith Smedley. A monster that can hid amongst the people. This is the very creature that he sought. He had been led into a trap. No to be outdone Keith pulled the handgun from his coat at pointed it directly at the chest of the man before him.

“You didn’t really think that I would come alone and unarmed, did you? If you had not somehow disposed of the note that you wrote me, then I may have been more inclined to think of you as a frightened informer. But stealing the note from my office? Well, that just made me think of all sorts of outcomes to this meeting. And this is the one where I shoot you and the ensuing autopsy reveals that you are a monster of origins unknown and was formerly terrifying the locals before being dispatched by me.”

Samuel Gates put up his arms in a gesture of surrender. He did not look particularly defeated, which bothered Smedley.

“What are you? Why are you here? Why did you kill Albert Brawnly and Christian Mayweather, and the miners? What part did you have to play in that?”

Keith's barrage of questions was forceful. He was determined to get the answers that he desired. Samuel Gates face dissolved back into that of Benjamin Brigges.

"I can honestly say that I had very little to do with the first death here in Matlock. Albert Brawnly you say? I admit that I did pursue him, but I was feeling out of sorts and simply couldn't catch up with him. Pity about that nasty fall from the cliff side walking track. He looked quite tasty". Brigges again gave that malevolent smile.

The horror of what was being said sent shivers through Smedley. This thing wanted to eat Albert Brawnly; hideous. The fact that the creature had admitted that he ultimately was not responsible for the man's death was lost in the realisation of what this beast wanted to do.

"And Christian Mayweather?" Smedley said shaking the pistol threateningly.

"Pity about that poor soul. He was so completely frightened of me that he threw himself off the cliff rather than allow me to eat him. What a nerve!?" Brigges forced indignation made Smedley's stomach turn.

"Which is basically what I thought had happened to you my dear Mister Smedley. How did you survive the fall by the way? I would really like to know? It came as quite a surprise to me to discover that you were still alive and raising all sorts of hell about me in the Town Hall."

The questions from the monster caught Smedley off guard. As the one holding the gun he should have felt under absolutely no obligation to answer. But there was a genuine note of curiosity from the thing. It subconsciously appealed enough to Smedley to provide answers.

“I managed to grab onto the Orange Trumpet Vines growing down the cliff-face. As strong as ropes those things”. His brief answer gave away none of the bravery and audacity of his cunning self-devised and executed rescue from the monster.

“Very clever Mister Smedley. I cannot help but be impressed”

“The miners, tell me about the miners!” Keith was irritated. The murderous thing complimenting him was somehow abrasive.

“Ah, yes, the miners. Well, you really must forgive me Mister Smedley, occasionally I lose my self-control and go on a feeding-frenzy. As happened in the mine. But I cannot take all the credit. I had help in the covering up of my little indiscretion.”

“The dynamite; you mean? It helped you cover up the…..deaths? Or do you mean that you can hide effectively in amongst us. Is that it?” Smedley was not quick enough on the uptake. He had not considered the option of an accomplice.

“No, that’s not what I mean at all?” said Brigges.

Smedley was still contemplating what was being said. Unheard behind him Mayor Tremorlund was creeping up on him, shoes off, to ensure stealth.

"Well, this has been enjoyable, but as they say all good things must come to an end. And your end is in sight Mister Smedley. I have decided to settle down here in Matlock, at least for the foreseeable future. It has everything that I need. And, I simply cannot have you making things difficult for me." Brigges tone was ominous.

A thought now occurred to Keith. What if this thing had had help all along? There was a willing accomplice of some description. As the thought ran through his head a large spanner came down with a crushing blow on the back of Smedley's head.

He was obliterated into unconsciousness immediately. He dropped the gun which clattered along the stone floor. He joined it there in a crumpled mess.

"Thank you, Thaddeus; a job well done. Now let's make it look like a tragic accident, shall we?"

Chapter 20: The Cable-Car Tram

Smedley's head hurt; it hurt like it never had before. He could feel rain upon his face and cold wet cobblestones beneath his back. He managed with great effort to open his eyes. It was dark. He attempted to move but a searing pain shot through his head further inflaming the agony he was suffering.

There was a noise too. It was both familiar and unfamiliar at the same time. He couldn't concentrate enough to identify what it was, or where he was. All that he wanted was for the pain in his head to ease.

Like lightening he remembered recent events. He had a gun pointing at the creature. Where was it? He patted is coat pockets. He could not find it. He was in the Chapel, but not anymore. Now he was outside. He turned his head. He was lying on the ground. It looked to be the main road; Bank Street.

The noise that had pervaded his consciousness was becoming louder. He tried to get up but was again stopped by the pain. Instead he managed to turn his head in the opposite direction so that he could see where the sound was coming from. Through the gloom he could make out a cable-car tram moving relentlessly toward him. In a flash of realisation, he recognised that he was lying on the track directly in the path of the oncoming car.

With a herculean effort and disregarding the pain he was in; he heaved himself up into a sitting position. The car was barely ten feet away from him. He pushed himself along the ground trying to will his legs and body into action. But his limbs seemed to resist. Five feet away; Smedley realised with horror that he was in the middle of the section of track that split into two. If one of the cars was approaching from this direction, then……

He turned his neck, the other tram car was as close to him but coming at him from the opposite direction. Instinct and adrenalin took over. Ignoring the agony that he was suffering he jumped up and out of the way just clipping the car coming down the steep hill as it passed him.

His mind raced. There was nobody on either of the cars. The operator, the monster must be running the cars from the control shed at the bottom of the hill, in Crown square.

'You'll have to get up earlier than that to take me out of the picture' thought Smedley. He ran along the dual section of track. Catching up with the ascending car he mounted the empty double deck tram. This would take him safely away from the creature and back up the hill toward the main hydro establishments in the town. He would be safe there.

Rain began to fall in buckets. It was heavy. The floor of the car was already wet from the previous rainfall. Smedley wondered where the crew were that was working on the system earlier. But he didn't know how long he had been unconscious. They may have left for their homes and accommodations a long time ago for all he knew.

The tram was reaching the section where it went back onto a single part of track for the final ascension to the top of the road. He did not realise that his footing was not secure on the wet floor. The car jerked onto the section of track. Smedley stumbled and slipped on the floor. He came crashing down. He didn't even realise it, but he was unconscious once more.

***

If he had been able to think clearly about it; Keith Smedley would have known exactly how long a time he lay aboard the tram car in an unconscious state. He woke up. He was still on the tram. But it was not climbing anymore. It was on the downhill run. In fact, it had just entered the split section of track marking the very middle of the system where both cars pass each other. This is where he had narrowly avoided his own demise only a short time ago. He managed to stand up and survey his surroundings more carefully.

He could see the approaching cable tram car. Captain Benjamin Brigges was aboard at the front wearing a maniacal expression on his assumed human face. He must have found out that his plan to assassinate Smedley had failed and caught the tram up the hill to finish the job himself.

It started to rain; not just little but a lot. It added to the growing terror inside Smedley. The cars approached each other. Keith ran up the tiny curving staircase to the open top level. The rain was now torrential. It made visibility nearly impossible. But more than that, it would ensure that nobody would be around on Bank street to see what was happening. He was alone.

Something else was wrong as well. The speed of the tram was far in excess of anything that he had seen during it's initial testing before. It was meant to be a casual ride both up and down the hill. But the creature must have pushed the speed of the car up to the maximum. Keith knew that if he tried to dismount the car at this speed he may well suffer a life-threatening injury.

The entire situation was ironic. If he jumped off, he may well die. If he stayed aboard he would most certainly be attacked by the thing. The cars were about to begin passing each other. Brigges was preparing to jump from the front drivers chair to the front entry way on the descending car. He watched through the driving rain as Brigges leapt across like a death-defying circus trapeze performer. The creature was aboard his car now. Any second now he would make his way down the centre isle of the car and scurry up the rear stairs toward him. Smedley had run out of time.

The speed at which the cars would pass would preclude him from having another attempt at escape. He judged the distance between the top of the two cars and hurled himself toward the open aired roof-top seating on the opposing car. The hand-rail area that he had pushed from was slippery. His shoes did not have sufficient grip and they slipped out from beneath him, stealing from him the majority of the force he put into the jump. His arms were flailing but they managed to catch the rail of the passing car and he held on for dear life.

He looked down; the ground was almost a blur. He felt panic rise within him. He may not have sufficient grip to hold on. If he fell now, he could easily be dragged beneath the steel wheels of the cable-car and cut into pieces.

Keith tried his best to rearrange his grip to climb aboard the tram properly. He was vaguely aware of a movement beside him. Brigges had jumped from the descending car back onto the ascending one along with him. No matter how he tried, Keith couldn't get a proper grip, not enough to pull himself up.

A face appeared above him. It was Brigges. He was laughing with malevolence.

"Tragically killed by the cable car on a rainy night. Nobody could possibly think that was anything other than an accident. You've been a very engaging opponent Mister Keith Smedley, but now it is time for you to DIE!"

He shouted the final word safe in the knowledge that the rain was so hard nobody would hear it. It fell with such force that nobody in the shops or houses along bank road would even see them. Keith was about to lose his life.

His feet kicked around looking for a grip of some kind. His knees could feel the emptiness of the window that he was straddling. It led to the lower section of the car. This window was in the slid-down position.

Brigges mercilessly gripped Smedley's hands and began to forcefully loosen his grip on the handrail. Keith managed to twist his legs into a position whereby he could push them through the small window. Just as Brigges was about to send Smedley crashing to the hard-paved ground below whilst travelling at break-neck speed, Keith pushed away from Brigges and manoeuvred his body through the window. He landed with a thump in the seat occupying the space beside the window.

Smedley was amazed, he had actually managed to cheat death. The roar of anger and frustration he heard through the rain from above, reminded him that he was in no way out of danger. Loud footsteps could be heard running along the short top deck of the car.

"There must be a brake?" he said to himself aloud. He looked around. The drivers seat was in plain view. He clambered out of the seat and ran to the driver's seat. To his absolute amazement there was an old woman sitting in the chair. He had not seen her when he looked before, or even when he approached. Suddenly she was just there. She looked familiar, but Keith was so surprised to see her that he couldn't think straight.

She didn't say anything but indicated to her face and then mouth and then pointed in the direction of the creature scurrying down the back stairs. She managed to do this twice before necessity forced Keith to turn around. Brigges was there he was barely five feet away.

The sudden appearance of the woman had thwarted his plan to apply the brake and dismount the tram. He glanced back at the driver's chair. It was empty.

"There is no help for you know my troublesome mister Smedley!" growled Brigges.

In a flash of realisation, Keith new exactly who the woman was that he had seen. The one now unbelievably no longer there.

"Madam Alice Athalia, Psychic to the crowned heads of Europe" Keith repeated the introduction that Martha Morrell had given him when he inquired as to who the photograph was on the table, on the night of the second séance.

The name had an immediate and uninterpretable effect upon Brigges. He stopped dead in his tracks.

"What did you say?" he demanded; his face twisting in anger.

"You should tell me Captain Brigges, or is it Samuel Gates; who are you really?" Keith was stalling for time. He needed an escape plan, or he would most surely be murdered at the hands of this beast.

To his horror the body, face and clothes of Brigges dissolved and reformed into that of Madam Athalia. She stood before him; not the kindly expression that he had seen in her photo, but a sadistic look upon her wizened old face.

"I absorbed every inch of that wretched woman hoping to inherit her psychic abilities; nothing. She cheated me!"

Keith looked at the entry way to the tram. They were still travelling too fast for him to jump off. But he was prepared to risk it.

"That's the problem with Psychics Brigges; they never really disappear. She has been helping us against you all along". Keith's ruse to gain more time struck a nerve with the monster.

"That witch! I'll kill.........." The threat was redundant. How do you kill somebody that is already dead?

"From the great beyond; guiding us in the way to bring about your eventual defeat. That's what she is doing. And what exactly are you going to do about it? Kill her?"

The tables had turned. Now it was Smedley that had the mocking tone. This enraged the monster. She dissolved and turned once more into Benjamin Brigges.

"Tell me what she has said! Tell me what she knows? Or I will rip if from your body piece by piece!" the threat sent a shudder of cold through Smedley. He had to stall for more time. He backed away one step. Keith looked firstly at the driver's seat and then at the doorway. Sensing his desire to perhaps jump rather than face him the creature laughed.

"Still going way too fast Smedley. If you jump you will deliver the *accidental* death that I so desire for you. If you stay you had better answer my questions or I will rip you into shreds until you do, and then find a way to cover up the sudden disappearance of poor Mister Keith Smedley".

Neither choice was palatable for Keith. The rain had begun to ease. He could tell that they were approaching the juncture of Smedley street; named after the original founder of Smedley's hydro.

A thought of inspiration; all he needed to do was distract the beast for a second. That is all that he needed.

"The trouble with spirits from the other side, is that they have a habit of appearing where and when you least expect them" said Keith rather mysteriously.

"Meaning; what?" snarled Brigges.

"Captain Benjamin Brigges; may I present Madam Alice Athalia" Keith indicated that the old woman was standing behind him. Brigges fell for the ruse. He turned expecting to see the ghost of the old woman standing behind him. There was nobody.

Keith used the precious time to lunge for the brake and pulled it with all of his might. The cable-car tram screeched in response and lost most of its speed in the next second. Brigges and Smedley were knocked off their feet by the sudden deceleration.

Both were scampering to their feet, but Smedley was faster, and nearer to the door. He ran. There was a howl of anger behind him. Keith had Smedley's hydro in sight. It's imposing stone walls and ornate windows and wrought-iron work just visible in the lessening gloom of the receding rain.

Nothing was going to stop him reaching the safety of the business that he managed. Keith Smedley ran faster than he had ever done before. He daren't look around because he knew that the beast would be in pursuit. The entrance was tantalisingly close. As he looked the main door opened and three people emerged. He didn't recognise who they were but was overjoyed to see them.

He ran up the short pathway to the main door. They parted to allow him entry to the covered awning keeping the rain off them.

"Oh, Mister Smedley, no umbrella?" asked one of the trio.

"I got caught in the downpour" he said looking behind him. There was nothing but the empty street. He was puffed. The he added

"I thought that there was somebody behind me; did you see anyone?"

The trio shook their heads and indicated to the contrary.

"I must have been mistaken" he said to finalise the subject.

"Well, gather your strength, it looks like the rain is backing off now. And we are off to the King's Tavern for a nightcap. Would you care to join us?"

"Thank you that is very kind, but I think that I'll go inside and dry off and get some work done." He replied.

"Very well then, off we go" with that the trio left the safety of the awning and with umbrellas raised marched down the pathway to the road.

Smedley watched them leave. If the creature was there he could raise the alarm, but he guessed that it wasn't. It was clear to Smedley now that the monster wanted to secret itself into the township of Matlock. And people like himself, were preventing that from happening.

This was a battle of wits as much as a physical battle. If he couldn't find a way to expose or rid Matlock of the monster, then it would only be a matter of time before the thing got rid of him.

The trio of guests turned left at Bank Road where it becomes Rutland Street. The King's Tavern was only a short way up. They would be safe for sure.

Keith pondered the recent attempt on his life. If it hadn't been for an unexpected appearance of a ghost, then the creature would have surely succeeded. He must let Martha know of these events.

Then it occurred to him. The creature must have an accomplice. Who else would have knocked him unconscious in the Chapel? What kind of person would consort with an inhuman creature like that?

But then a further unsettling thought occurred to him. Where was his gun? It was in his hand when he was knocked unconscious; now it was nowhere to be seen. Should he report it as missing to the Police? He dismissed the idea almost as immediately as he thought of it. How would he explain why he was in the Wesleyan Chapel with a hand pistol? He tried to come up with a multitude of other reasons that he was carrying his gun and it became lost, but they all seemed hollow and unconvincing. He was trapped by gall of the person or thing that had taken it from him.

***

Keith Smedley reflected on everything that had happened since the first sighting of the monster. He was in the staff dining room. It was safer here. This part of the building always had somebody coming or going or enjoying a cup of tea between conducting therapy sessions or the like.

One figure kept reoccurring in the recounting of events in his mind. One person had been vehemently opposed to conducting a search for the creature. Or even to acknowledge its existence. And all the beast needed was one accomplice to help it secret itself into society. Someone of significant influence and standing in the community.

"Mayor Thaddeus Tremorlund" he said aloud.

Chapter 21: Thursday 16th March 1893

The Rockside Hydropathic Establishment was six stories high at its tallest points. They were the two castle-like turrets that jutted out at its front overlooking the steep downward valley of houses and businesses below it. It may have even been able to be mistaken for a castle owing to its appearance except for the large Edwardian windows scattered evenly throughout its façade.

Keith Smedley had arranged to meet with William Aitkens there, the owner. Aitkens had a much grander office than Keith's. Larger, wood panelling, a full-sized fire place rather than the small half-sized one in Keith's office. The desk was larger, it all just appeared to be more opulent overall.

William stood up to greet Keith as he was led in by a member of the Rockside staff.

"Good to see you Keith, please come in and sit down; make yourself comfortable. Can I get you a drink of some description?' William dismissed the staff member with a thankyou, and pointed to the liquor cabinet. It was barely noon, so Keith declined.

"Too early for me; but please go ahead if you would like"

"Never drink alone Keith; something my father taught me as a younger man" He settled himself back into his large green studded chesterfield desk chair and smiled.

“How may I be of assistance today. An overbooking at Smedley’s that I can take off your hands maybe?”

It was wishful thinking on William’s part. Although both hydro establishments were the largest and most popular in town, they were rarely at absolutely full capacity.

“I wanted to talk about the Monster of Matlock” said Keith simply.

“Oh; that” William responded his smile fading.

“Before you stop me William, you have known me for as long as I have been in Matlock running Smedley’s in place of its original founder. You know me to not be impulsive nor prone to fanciful notions”. Keith sought to head-off any dismissive thoughts from William straight-up.

Well; that is true, I suppose” replied William half-heartedly. He clearly did not want to discuss the Monster at all.

“Please do me the honour of listening to what I have to say without bias or prejudice.” The call to his sense of honour clearly appealed to William and he nodded in acquiescence and altered his tone accordingly.

“Very well, Keith, I shall. What do you have to tell me”.

Keith relayed the recent events to William.

“Somebody wrote me an anonymous note; which unsurprisingly disappeared from my office shortly thereafter. It said that they had absolute proof that the monster existed and could supply a sample for scientific evaluation. I was to meet them last night at the Wesleyan Chapel. I dutifully showed up at the appointed time and was confronted by the thing itself, in human form."

Keith reached a natural break in his retelling of events. William's eyebrows shot upwards, but he did not disparage his friend, nor did he interrupt. Keith continued.

"He called himself Captain Benjamin Brigges of the Mary Celeste. But then transformed right before my eyes into a Police Inspector from London by name of Samuel Gates. The most extraordinary thing that I ever seen with my own eyes."

Once more William seemed to be resisting intervening.

"Go on?" he encouraged.

"He, or rather *it*, wants to live amongst us and sustain its ungodly existence by feeding people. I can only assume those poor victims will be strangers that pass through. Travellers or other people that won't be missed. That is what it does William, it nourishes itself on human meat."

The shocking revelation should have garnered an objection from William, but it did not. He indicated that Keith should proceed with any further information.

"I thought that I had outsmarted it. I brought with me my pistol. Pointing it at the chest of the thing I stupidly thought that I had it under my control?"

"What happened" asked William leaning forward in his chair unable to hide his curiosity.

"Somebody came up from behind and knocked me unconscious. I awoke on the tracks of the cable-car tram moments before it would have sliced me into pieces!" Keith didn't realise it, but his voice had become raised and his words spoken faster.

"You got out of harm's way?" William rhetorical question was responded to.

"Yes, I mounted the car hoping to catch a free ride back up the hill to Smedley`s, but I slipped and rendered myself unconscious again. When I awoke the car was travelling at break-neck speed and the I was on the descending journey. The creature was in the opposing car coming at me!"

William's eyes widened as he got swept up in the narrative.

"It jumped onto my car, but I managed to escape by jumping onto his. Realising the ruse, it pursued me. Thankfully, I used the driver's brake and halted the journey and made good my escape safely back to Smedley's"

Keith finished off his abridged version of events. William seemed a little disappointed that the climax of the story was so brief.

"Did it chase you?" asked Aitkens.

"No, but I couldn't tell you why; I am just glad to be alive William" replied Smedley.

William put his index fingers together and rested them on his chin, contemplating the story.

"Who knocked you out in the Chapel, did you see?" Williams question was clearly seeking more detail about the story rather than criticising it; this pleased Keith.

“No, I didn’t see, but that brings me to why I am here” Keith said.

This puzzled William.

“I assumed that you were here to tell me about your scrape with death last night?” inquired William.

“That’s not as important as who it is that is assisting the creature. It has to be one of us; one of the townsfolk. Somebody that stands to lose the most from exposing the creature as real. Imagine what would happen to our town if it was known that a creature lurked here somewhere.?” Keith’s question was leading William, but William did not show any sign of knowing that he was being corralled into a conclusion.

“It would be an absolute circus. People would come from miles around to hunt the thing down. It would be good for business. We would scarcely have room for everyone. Imagine that Keith, one-hundred percent capacity? It would be heavenly! Well, at least for as long as it lasted of course” William seemed to be lost in the idea of how it would affect him in a good way.

“I’m sure that it wouldn’t last forever” responded Keith.

“No, such things never do. Look at the legend of the Loch Ness Monster? What poppycock! It certainly never led me to want to explore the Scottish Highlands. I suppose in the long-term the name of Matlock would be tarnished forever as the Monster capital of Derbyshire.” William was walking directly toward the realisation that Keith wanted him to.

“Mayor Tremorlund wouldn’t like that! Not one bit” he said in conclusion.

“No, William he wouldn’t. I am certain that he would do everything in his power to ensure that it doesn’t happen. Anything and everything” his ominous words held meaning. William reacted.

“You don’t think that Thaddeus is in cahoots with this thing, do you?”

“That is exactly what I think William” he confirmed.

William looked as if he was about to object and then thought the better of it. He took his time to contemplate matters before speaking again.

“If we assume that the monster really *does* exist? And if we take for granted that it wants to live here furtively, then I suppose the answer is yes; it would need an accomplice of some standing to help it cover-up any indiscretions, like killing and eating one of us.” As absurd as it sounded, the logic was secure.

“That is twice now that you have seen this creature Keith. I think that for the sake of everyone, that I should believe you and offer my assistance” William’s words were unexpected. Keith assumed that he would need to do a lot more convincing.

“Thank you, William, that means a lot to me” Keith said, clearly relieved.

“I’ve just had a thought. It was the mayor that found the miners shortly after their tragedy.” William looked to Keith for his thoughts on the matter.

“What if the monster had been there causing mayhem. How better to cover up the deaths than with a stick of dynamite that someone manages to light at the wrong end of the fuse. You know how experienced the miners were with using dynamite. In the light of what you now know, do you actually believe that they were that careless?”

Keith presented his alternative way of thinking on the miner’s deaths.

“No; no, I do not. You are right of course. Mayor Thaddeus Tremorlund is beginning to look guiltier with each passing second.” William’s facial expression was sombre.

“What do we do?” William asked.

“We set a trap for him, and I have had an idea about exactly how to expose the Mayor as a traitor to the town and as a conspirator with an unholy daemon that needs to be vanquished from this life!” Keith’s words were resolute; he meant business.

“Have you told anybody else this?” asked William.

“Just you” he replied.

“Tell me what you are thinking? And let us plan together how best to tackle this problem?”

William was becoming enthused with the idea of exposing the Mayor. But it did look like he was still hedging his bets.

“It can’t be anything too dire; we must both face the possibility that you are wrong. All we have now is a working hypothesis. What we need is absolute proof before we accuse the Mayor of Matlock of anything inappropriate. Agreed?”

William's assertion was perfectly reasonable. He agreed to tread carefully in any plan composed to trick the Mayor into showing his true allegiances.

"What we have to come up with then, is a way to ensure that the Mayor tips his hand in such a way that he cannot squirm his way out of it. We will need witnesses, credible ones and the more the merrier" Keith laid out the basic groundwork for the blossoming plan.

"Alright then" agreed William. "Let's get to work!"

Chapter 22: A Future Plan

It took a good deal of convincing, but William had managed to talk Keith into waiting until the official opening of the cable-car tram on the 28th of March before enabling any plan to trap the Mayor. He had eventually agreed.

Keith knew that the Mayor would not want anything to sully the opening of the tram. Thaddeus had been an integral part of the opening ceremonies and surrounding semi-carnival proceedings.

Keith felt that he would be safe until then.

***

As expected the official opening of the cable car tram on Tuesday the 28th of March was a large-scale affair. From the size of the crowd it seemed that everyone from Matlock and the surrounding towns attended. The weather had mercifully warmed up enough so that it was possible to be outside without heavy clothing. Nobody knew how long it would last but they were happy that it coincided nicely with the celebration.

The Mayor predictably was in his element. Giving various speeches about the bright future of Matlock coming into the age of modern industry. Job Smith dedicated the tram that he had financed in its entirety to the town in the hopes that it helped the town continue to grow. As well as becoming a destination for travellers and holiday makers and new settlers.

The hot air balloon rides were very popular and the queue for them stretched for as longer than they could hope to service. The market building at the bottom of Bank road did a roaring trade that day. The stall holders all reported far above average sales.

Street performers had been hired from a troupe in London. It gave the celebrations a nice medieval touch. Various games were set up along the tram line. Bobbing for apples, a giant dart board game of skill using oversized darts that did not seem anywhere near as accurate as normal ones. Even pin the tail on the donkey was popular with the revellers. All in all, it was a great success. The thoughts of the recent deaths of two men followed by the tragic loss of the miners was nicely covered over by the celebrations.

The tram itself lived up to expectations, performing flawlessly the entire time, from the moment it was 'activated' by the cutting of a ribbon, to well into the night as the party-goers dissipated.

It was earlier though, during the height of the celebrations immediately following the noon launching of the tram that Martha, Michael and Keith were spotted talking together by Tiffany Tremorlund. She made it her business to secret herself near to them so that she could eves-drop on their conversation. Keith was speaking.

“We must get more information from Alice. The next séance is integral if we are to find the evidence we need to expose what is really happening here.”

“Patience Mister Smedley” said Martha “Soon it will be the full moon and we are assured of a connection with the spirit world. Alice will be able to point us directly to what we need.”

Keith nodded in agreement with the fact. One that he already knew. He was really just reassuring himself that the next séance would go ahead as planned this Saturday night. He had luckily decided to not take Martha and Michael into his confidence about drafting William Aitkens to aiding him expose the Mayor as the monster`s accomplice. Had he done so and Tiffany overhead any of it, his future plan to expose the mayor would have come asunder. But luck was on his side that afternoon.

Armed with the information about the forthcoming séance. Tiffany sidled her way through the crowd. She needed to let Thaddeus know the news as soon as she was able.

Chapter 23: Good Friday 31st March 1893

The cold weather had returned; snow had fallen lightly over the town. Martha was sitting in her favourite chair in the kitchen of Balmoral House. Michael was sitting opposite and was reading the paper. He put it down on the table and spoke to Martha who was doing some knitting.

"Do you think that it is gone? The monster, I mean."

"No, my dear; I fear that it is not. It is lurking somewhere here and is ready to pounce again. I don't know where or when, but you may be certain that it is still here, somewhere"

Martha's words were not unexpected, but Michael had held out the hope that the creature would just go away and leave them alone. It was too much to hope for.

"I suppose your right. I think that I'll retire for the evening" he said.

"I shall stay up for a short while and read the paper" Martha announced.

Michael arose from his chair and kissed Martha on the forehead, before leaving the kitchen. Martha put down her knitting and picked up the paper and looked over the various headlines of the stories printed on the front page. She chose one and began to read.

Outside a cloaked figure approached Balmoral House. He could see the lights at the front of the house were extinguished. There was a pathway around the side of the house. He gingerly walked along the snow-covered flagstones. The glass of the kitchen window could be seen clearly.

He peered through. Martha Morrell was there, sitting in a chair reading the paper. Michael Morell was nowhere in sight. The cloaked figure looked up at the first story of the building. A light was on in the main bedroom. That is surely where Michael would be at this time of evening he thought. The man crouched down ensuring that he did not put his foot in the flowerbed. It would leave a footprint in the soft soil, and he did not want to leave any markers behind. His purpose here was singular.

The snow began to fall again. Luck was on his side. By the time any alarm was raised it would cover his footprints along the stone pathway. It was almost as if the heavens were telling him that he would get away with his crime.

He pulled the gun from his coat pocket and regarded it in the light giving off from inside Balmoral House. Everything had fallen into place like it was meant to happen. And that is what he was telling himself. This was meant to happen. If he could just get rid of the troublesome Martha Morrell and by default Alice Athalia too, then there would be nobody to point an accusatory finger at him.

He took careful aim with the hand gun. Martha was sitting perfectly still. It was too easy. He cocked the hammer and reinsured that his aim was true. He had Martha's face in the raised sight at the end of the gun barrel. There would be no chance of surviving a gun shot to the head.

Looking around one last time to ensure that he was alone, and to reaffirm his escape route, he returned to aiming at his victim. She was once more in his sights. He squeezed the trigger. The gun bellowed a thunderous crack as it released the bullet. The diagonal lead harlequin style glass shattered. Just a single small pane of it. The noise and the kickback from the gun alarmed the murderer. He wasn't expecting it to be so loud and so forceful.

It took a second for him to compose himself enough to look at the results of the gunshot. Martha was slumped back in her chair the newspaper dropped against her chest. There was a single hole where her right eye should have been, oozing blood.

One more to be absolutely sure; he thought to himself. He took aim through the broken pane of glass and fired again. This time Martha's jaw was blown off, a sizeable section of it at least.

He could hear Michael calling down from the bedroom above.

"Martha, Martha what was that noise? Martha!"

She was most certainly dead and no longer a threat to the gunman. He made good his planned escape. His heart pounding, the noise of the two gunshots made his ears ring. He did not run as fast as he would have thought under the circumstances. It was more of a half-hearted sprint. But it was enough to ensure his escape.

***

Michael came running down the stairs as fast as he was able to at his age. He was still dressed not having had time to get into his pyjamas before the double explosion reached his ears. The entire time calling to Martha asking what had happened; wondering why she was not replying to him?

He came into the kitchen and saw her lying in the chair where he had left her only a short time before. The newspaper was covering her chest. Blood had splattered it. Martha's jaw was missing, an eye was missing, blood covered her face. He screamed. There was no thought of his own safety. No thought that a gunman might still be around nearby.

Michael simply couldn't make sense of it. What had happened? It looked like Martha had been shot, but from where? By whom? It took a while for the scene to make sense to him.

"I must get help!" he shouted loudly to an empty kitchen. He ran to the front door, unlocked it and flung it open. It was snowing. Out of sheer habit he reached for his overcoat on the coat rack by the front door and put it on. He didn't even register that he was doing so. Running out the front door he raced down the front pathway and stopped at the gate. It was slightly ajar. Not quite thinking why he pulled it open and froze. Where was he going to get help? Who should he raise the alarm too? The police station was in the centre of town. It would take him an hour to get there. What was closer?

Rockside Hydropathic; that is where he should go for help. He ran in the direction of his goal.

***

William Aitkens was working at his desk when a staff member flew in, flustered beyond compare.

"Mister Michael Morell from Balmoral House has come to us. His wife has been shot in her chair at home!" said the young man; his words blurring together.

"What?" asked Aitkens unable to comprehend what was just said.

"Martha Morell is dead. Shot in Balmoral House. Michael found the body" he said summarising events as he knew them once more.

"Dead? Martha Morell?" Aitkens was having trouble coming to terms with the news himself.

"He arrived in reception and told us what had happened. I was there along with Henry and James. Mister Morrell left to raise a further alarm. We don't know where he has gone?" said the young man. Aitkens was scrambling to think what to do.

"Joseph, take Henry and James and go to Balmoral house and find out what has happened. When you know for sure come back to me. I will send for the police and have them go directly to Balmoral House!" Joseph nodded his compliance with the instructions and raced from the room.

***

Joseph Rowlett, Henry Bradshawe and James Green ran to Balmoral House. They opened the gate and ran to the front door. But there they stopped.

“Should we go in?” asked Henry of his companions.

They were unsure. It would be unseemly to not be invited in by the house owner. But this was an emergency; surely, they should not stand upon ceremony.

“Where did he go?” asked James

“Mister Morrell? I don’t know. To raise a further alarm, he said” responded Joseph.

“Let’s go around the side” suggested Henry.

This was something that they could all agree upon. They left the front door and took the side path to the kitchen windows at the rear of the house. The snow was beginning to fall quite heavily now. Leaning forward they could see the body of Martha in her chair, bloodied and lifeless.

The noise of the front gate to Balmoral House being flung open alerted them to the presence of someone.

“Let’s see who it is?” said James. Their bravery enforced by their numbers, the three young men made their way back to the front of the house. It was Michael Morrell that they saw coming down the pathway. Joseph called out to him.

“Mister Morrell, we can see your wife though the window”

Michael indicated that they should follow him inside. He unlatched the large oak door and swung it open. He was still very clearly upset.

“Where did you go after to you left Rockside?” inquired Joseph as they moved through the house toward the kitchen.

“The neighbours; they’ve gone for the police” he said.

The remainder of the short journey down the main hall and past the stairs into the kitchen was done in silence. They all entered the kitchen. Martha could be clearly seen in the light of the lantern beside her chair. Bloodied and without question shot through the face.

“I heard an explosion” said Michael weakly.

The three young men all gathered around Martha’s lifeless body. They looked around. Up and down and then back at Michael.

“There is no sign of a lamp explosion” observed Henry.

“Do you have a gun in the house, a hunting rifle or something other?” inquired James. Michael shook his head indicating that there were no weapons in the house at all.

The obvious and inescapable conclusion was that somebody has deliberately shot Martha Morrell.

“There is no sign that there was a struggle. It looks like Missus Morrell was reading the paper in her chair and a shot or two was fired at her. But why? Who? How?” Joseph was asking the obvious questions. The ones that nobody had immediate answers to.

“Look over here” said James garnering their attention. He was pointing at the kitchen window. A single frame of the diamond shaped glass was broken. The three young men gathered around it looking. Michael remained with Martha looking at her in disbelief of what had happened.

It was clear to the other three that a bullet or two must have come through the smashed window pane and hit Martha. They looked through the window. And back at Martha.

“Can you see anything outside?” inquired James of his compatriots.

“Nothing, too much snow has fallen. If there was anything it is covered up by now” answered Joseph. Indeed, it had begun to snow even more heavily than before. If there was any evidence outside to point to who and what had occurred, it was being erased by mother nature.

***

At about quarter to eleven, William Aitkens arrived with two other men in tow. It was Mister Jesse Davies, the head of the nearby Poplar Cottage hydropathic establishment, and Mister Brian Statham, the town baker. He was a resident in Rutland Street.

They all exchanged only cursory greetings under the strange circumstances. The sight of Martha’s body bloodied, and missing part of her jaw was shocking. William took it upon himself to ask the obvious question.

“Michael what happened?” but then realising that perhaps the broad nature of the question, revised it.

“Michael, exactly what happened from the last time that you saw Martha alive?”

All eyes turned to Michael.

“I put down the paper. Martha was knitting. I said that I was going to retire for the evening. Martha said that she would stay up for a short time and read the paper. I retired to our bedroom. I had barely began undoing my waistcoat when I heard an explosion. I called out to Martha asking what it was? But she didn’t reply. I went downstairs and found her like this? I think there may have been a second explosion, but now I’m not so sure. I can’t think clearly.”

His summation of the events was now detailed for the six bystanders.

“Look over here” indicated Joseph indicating to the broken pane of glass. Fragments of which were inside the kitchen.

“This must have been where the bullet came in; but who?” William was putting into words what they were all thinking. Further conversation was interrupted by the arrival of the police.

They had brazenly marched into the house without any announcement of any sort. Which was understandable. Sargent Ramshall and Police Constables Wilson and Harrison took in the scene before them. Sargent Ramshall taking immediate charge of the situation.

“I think that under the circumstances we should keep you in clear sight at all times Mister Morrell, you understand of course. We have an investigation to undertake to find out what has happened here tonight. Constable Harrison, please take Mister Morrell to his room until such time as he can be properly questioned.”

The Police Constable moved toward Michael Morrell and took him gently by the elbow. Unable or unwilling to object Michael obeyed without question. He was led away.

“Who was first on the scene?” he asked of the remaining men.

“We were Sargent” Joseph indicated himself, Henry and James.

“We came up to the house when Mister Morrell alerted us at the Rockside, we didn’t come in but went around the side and could see poor old Martha in her chair; shot in the head. Mister Morrell arrived, and we came into the kitchen then”

Joseph explainted what had happened. Then the Sargent wanted to know about William, Brian and Jesse. They told him their involvement in the events.

“This is going to be a tricky one” said the Sargent at the end of everybody`s recounting of events. He scratched his head, taking off his helmet in order to do so. He looked around at the scene as it was described by the men, taking note of the broken glass, the lack of any footprints outside owing to the falling snow and looked like he reached a decision of some kind.

“There is nothing else to do at this point. Captain Wiksworth will be informed, and he will without doubt send for Superintendent Lyle. The sooner that this matter is investigated fully, the sooner we may get to the bottom of what has happened here”.

***

It was well past midnight by the time Captain Perry Wiksworth arrived. He insisted upon questioning Michael Morrell himself. And then when Superintendent Lyle finally arrived closer to 1:30am; Michael Morrell was questioned again.

A search was initiated at the Superintendent`s behest of the house and grounds. The primary goal was to uncover the weapon that had been used in the cold-blooded murder of Martha Morrell. The search was to also uncover any evidence of who may have perpetrated such a heinous crime. The snowfall however had ensured that no such physical evidence was found.

Chapter 24: Easter Saturday 1st April 1893

It had been a difficult night. The complete lack of any physical evidence other than the body of Martha Morrell had been frustrating Captain Perry Wiksworth. In the early hours of the morning before sunrise, Martha had been moved to the mortuary section of the local hospital. Both Doctor Moxton and the Coroner Sidney Taylor had inspected the body together. Doctor Moxton removing a bullet from inside the brain directly behind the eye where the bullet had penetrated.

Captain Wiksworth's men had uncovered the other bullet, the one that would have taken off part of the jaw, in the wall behind where the body was found. It was ascertained that they were of the same calibre and pointed to a hand gun that would have been capable and suitable for firing that kind of ammunition.

***

It was about 11:00am when the Mister James Potter, the magistrate's clerk and his assistant Mister Gill arrived so as to further interview Michael Morrell. They walked up the street towards Balmoral House along with two well-dressed young ladies. Neither of the men recognised the young women. They were perhaps in their early twenties. The two gentlemen rightly supposing that they had arrived on one of the morning trains. It soon became apparent that they too were making their way to Balmoral House. They all met at the front gate. Hats were removed as James Potter introduced himself and his assistant and they inquired as to the identity of the two women.

"I am Davinia Davies, and this is my sister Emily. We are here to visit Uncle Michael and Aunt Martha. We're staying for Easter and returning home next week" said the elder one. Still puzzled as to why these two men were there.

"Why are you here mister Potter?" asked Emily politely.

"You haven't heard?" said James nervously looking at his assistant.

"Heard what? We've only just arrived by train from Manchester" stated Davinia.

"Oh, no, this is terrible. I don't know what to say..." James Potter was at a loss for words. He was in the unfortunate position to have to tell Martha's nieces of her demise.

"So, you're nieces on your Aunt's side of the family" interjected Mister Gill skirting around the subject.

"No, Uncle Michael is my father's brother. Aunt Martha has no living relatives that we know of. What is all this about please gentlemen, somebody tell us what has happened?" Davinia and Emily were clearly becoming increasingly upset.

There was nothing to it, they simply had to be told, thought James Potter.

"It is my sad duty to inform you that your Aunty, Martha Morrell was killed last night. Death by shooting. We don't know who by?"

There was a stunned silence from both young ladies as they grappled with the news.

"Uncle Michael; is he here?" Emily was at the point of tears.

"Yes, yes, he is inside; no doubt with one of the Constables. We are from the magistrate`s office, here to question him about the events of last night".

He opened the gate to allow the ladies entry. They scurried to the front door still unable to contemplate what they had just been told.

"It is fortunate that you are both here; Michael is in quite a state and will benefit from having some family around him" Mister Gill's observation went unacknowledged.

***

James Potter and Gerard Gill had gone ahead with their interview of Michael Morrell. However, it had not turned up any new insights. All that was known seemed to have been gleaned from Michael. Now that some time had passed he had had time to fully realise that Martha was dead. He had broken down a number of times during the night and the next morning. He was a widower. His wife of as many years as he could remember had been cruelly taken from him. It was very sad.

Captain Wiksworth and Superintendent Lyle were at the Police station in Matlock awaiting the results of the inspection of the body by the Corner and the Doctor.

"No footprints in the garden bed beside the window. Indicating that whoever it was stood upon, or even couched down on the stone footpath; took aim and fired"

Captain Wiksworth went over the reconstruction of the murder as best as could be explained.

The obvious suspect in this instance, was of course Michael Morrell. But there was no motive. William Aitkens had known Michael and Martha for the past fifteen years and never known them to say a harsh word to each other. They appeared to be, for all intents and purposes, a happily-married retired couple.

Superintendent Lyle voiced his viewpoint.

"Even if it was Michael Morrell, for whatever reason. He would have had to leave Martha in the kitchen, retrieve a firearm, go outside and walk around the side of the house taking aim through the kitchen window and shoot. It doesn't make any sense. The open front door would have alerted Martha to the cold running through the house and she most surely would have investigated, and not been sitting in her chair reading the paper".

Captain Perry Wiksworth agreed with the Superintendent.

"We've sent for Elizabeth Lister, the Morrell's charlady. She should be here presently. Hopefully she can bring to light a new fact that can help us."

Anything and everything that they could do as the investigators was on the table. A brazen murder by shooting in Matlock. It simply was never heard of before. Neither of the men had the recent miner's deaths, nor the tragic deaths of Christian Mayweather or Albert Brawnly in mind. To them, there was absolutely no connection between last-night's shooting, and the tragic events of the last few weeks.

"I wonder if the date has significance?" quipped Captain Wiksworth.

"What do you mean?" asked Lyle.

"Good Friday; Easter Friday, the thirty-first of March. I wonder if it had any bearing on the murder? If we knew that, maybe we would be closer to knowing why anyone would shoot an apparently harmless old lady?"

Any further conjecture was interrupted by the arrival of the Morrell's charlady Elizabeth Lister. She was clearly very flustered. Handkerchief pushed up to her nose and mouth.

"Please come in and sit-down Missus Lister" Captain Wiksworth indicated that she should take the chair on the opposite side of his desk. The constable that had fetched Missus Lister from her home was dismissed with a wave of Perry's hand.

"Terrible business" said the Superintendent by way of acknowledging how upset Elizabeth was.

"I cannot believe it; simply cannot believe it at all. This is awful" blubbered Elizabeth through her hanky.

"Please try to compose yourself Missus Lister. We have a few questions, that's all" assured Perry.

"I shall try" responded Elizabeth half-heartedly.

“Can you describe the last time that you were at Balmoral house for us please. Leave out no detail however unimportant you may think it to be” Perry’s question had a calming effect on the woman. She seemed to gather herself as she prepared to answer it.

“I arrived at Balmoral House around four o’clock in the afternoon. I did the cleaning. It took quite some time. The rugs, the fireplaces, the dusting. You’ve seen it, the place is huge. Far too big for just the two of them. But I know that they love it anyway”

Elizbeth was on the verge of crying again but managed to avert it and continue her account of events.

“With the cleaning done. I prepared the meal for the couple. That was around six-pm. It was a beef wellington. So, it took a bit of time to prepare and then into the oven and it was done about seven-thirty. I laid out the table, not the large dining room table you see the small one in the kitchen; that is where they preferred to eat. Nice and intimate you see. Oh, and then what. They preferred to clean up themselves after dinner, I didn’t have to wait around for them. And I had my own husband’s tea to prepare. I left them to it. I recall that the clock in the hallway had just begun to strike eight o’clock when I left. And that was the last time that I saw poor Martha alive”

It was too late to avert a new round of crying. Perry Wiksworth and Lyle allowed her the emotional outburst before continuing with their questions. Superintendent Lyle this time.

“Do you know of anyone that may have wished Martha any harm?”

It was an obvious question, but one that needed to be answered by as many of the Morrell’s friends as possible in order to glean some insight into the case. For her part, Elizabeth seemed to give the question quite a good deal of thought before replying.

“No, I can’t…unless you think that…..”

“What is it Missus Lister?” pushed Superintendent Lyle.

“The full moon tonight, you see that was required. Martha was telling me. It couldn’t be done safely at any other time”

The half-explanation did nothing to lift the veil on what Elizabeth was referring to. She could see the blank look on their faces and offered more detail.

“The séance tonight to contact Madam Athalia on the spiritual plane. It was supposed to happen tonight. Because there was a full moon, it was the right time to do it. I didn’t have to be there because I knew that Michael’s nieces were visiting from Manchester. They would make up the numbers you see. And of course, Mister Smedley. That would have been more than enough to contact the dead.”

It should have come as more of a surprise to both of them that there was an other-worldly slant to the story; but Martha Morrell’s sister Madam Alice Athalia was still quite well known even though she had died about four years ago.

“I suppose that there could have been somebody that did not want the séance to go ahead. In case it uncovered anything to do with the recent deaths, the two men and all of the miners. Martha and Mister Smedley were determined to get to the bottom of the events. That is all that I can think of. Other than that Martha Morrell didn't have an enemy in the world. Who would wish her harm? Who would do something like this? It doesn't bear thinking about" Elizabeth was working up to another fit of crying.

"Keith Smedley; manager of Smedley's hydro?" queried Perry wanting to be absolutely sure of the identity of Martha's cohort in the séance.

"The very same" Elizabeth managed to say choking back further tears.

"I think that will do for now Missus Lister. Please be present at Balmoral House this afternoon at two-pm for the Coronial inquest" concluded Captain Wiksworth.

Perry indicated through his glass pane door that the constable should return and escort Elizabeth from the room. He did so. As Missus Lister left the room Perry and Lyle colluded on their new snippet of information.

"I think that we should have a word with Keith Smedley" stated Superintendent Lyle.

***

Keith Smedley was sitting in his office staring into thin air. The news of the shooting of Martha Morrell had spread through the town; he was completely numb. It had to be the séance he kept thinking to himself. The monster and the mayor couldn't let it go ahead for fear of what it may reveal. And without the paranormal abilities of Martha Morrell to call upon Alice Athalia, all was lost.

He was unaware of Superintendent Lyle and Captain Perry Wiksworth standing at his door for some time. They had been speaking to him, but it had not registered. Smedley shook himself into the present.

"I'm sorry gentlemen, what was that?" he asked.

"May we come in?" repeated Captain Wiksworth somewhat miffed at the lack of response from Smedley.

"Of course, please do" he said standing up and walking around his desk to shake their hands.

"How may I be of assistance?" Keith inquired as he showed them to seats. They sat, and Keith took his place behind his desk facing them.

"I shall take it that you are aware of recent events, so I'll begin with exactly why we've come to speak with you Mister Smedley. We are of the understanding that you and the recently deceased were to conduct a séance this evening? What was the aim of that encounter with the spirit-world?" The fact that Captain Wiksworth was inquiring about such a thing indicated that he took it seriously enough to warrant questioning.

Keith was a little flummoxed but composed himself enough to answer coherently and fully.

"Martha Morrell and I hoped to contact Madam Athalia and find out more about the recent deaths in Matlock. As you know, both Martha, Michael and I felt that we here in Matlock are being preyed upon by a creature that secretes itself amongst us. We wanted absolute proof so that we could take it to you, the authorities, so that you may act in the best interests of the town and the people of Matlock".

It was a magnanimous sentiment, albeit one tinged with the supernatural. Keith's viewpoints were widely known but somehow both Perry and Lyle had hoped that it would have waned with time and lack of evidence. Bizarrely Perry and Lyle could see that Smedley was in the same boat as them. All investigating strange goings-on in Matlock, all with the greater community in mind and at heart. They sympathised with him on that level at least.

Not really thinking of it, more of a reflex question, Superintendent Lyle asked Keith a question that sent a shudder through Keith's body.

"Do you own a handgun Mister Smedley?"

The monster and the mayor had him trapped. If he lied to the police and the handgun was found it would incriminate him. If he admitted to having a gun he may have to produce it. Keith was aware that he was taking too long to answer the question.

"Somewhere here. I would have to go and find it; but I couldn't tell you where it is at the moment" he said with obfuscated honesty.

"What type of bullet does it fire?" it was a logical follow-up question.

“I think a six or an eight, sparrow shot. I can’t quite remember. Why; is it important?”

Captain Wiksworth nodded.

“We don’t wish to leave any stone unturned in this investigation. You’ll understand of course”.

Keith was hoping against hope that they did not want him to front-up with the Colt revolver.

“If you could manage to find it and hand it in at the station for inspection that would be good” Captain Wiksworth had unknowingly trapped Smedley, but Keith did not want to show it.

“Yes of course, if you think that it will help?”

“It will” confirmed Lyle.

The authorities were reticent to delve deeper into the monster theory that was held by Smedley. That was to them, fanciful. But this was something concrete. A shooting had to have someone who used the gun. It was easier to concentrate upon a substantial case like this one, than give any credence to an unbelievable story like a monster haunting he town.

After some further routine questions like ‘when was the last time that you saw Martha Morrell?’ and ‘what did you speak of?’ and ‘did you know anyone that would want to cause the old woman any harm?’, and ‘where were you last night around ten-pm?’ the interrogation was over.

Smedley knew that he was holding back vital information from them. But they would never believe him; not without absolute proof. Keith suspected the Mayor. The murderer was in plain sight almost every day of the week. Yet he was untouchable. If Keith was correct in assuming that the Mayor was behind this murder, and that his gun was used in the killing, then he had effectively been implicated in the murder. His only saving grace was that his staff could account for Keith's presence in Smedley's at the time of the murder. It was small consolation, but a significant one.

The afternoon was approaching, and the Superintendent and Captain needed to be at the coronial inquest to be held at Balmoral House. They saw themselves out. Keith sat for a long time in his office feeling effectively trapped by the events. He had to find a way to expose the Mayor and the monster. His thoughts turned to the only man that had not completely dismissed the idea. William Aitkens of Rockside hydro.

***

The Coroner's inquest was held in the afternoon at Balmoral House in the dining room adjacent to the kitchen. As this was a criminal Coroner's hearing, a full jury was gathered of local men and they were sworn in. The foreman of the jury was Lawrence Wildgoose. The remaining members of the jury were Charles Yates, William Handcock, Thomas Bagshaw, William Statham, George Wragge, Joseph Boden, Joseph Raines, Arthur Farnesworth, John Tom-Wall, James Turner and Luke Bridge.

After the ceremony of swearing-in, Coroner Sidney Taylor addressed the session.

"It is my understanding that the family solicitor for the Morrells has been sent for and as such it would be prudent for this inquest to await his arrival from London. The purpose of today will be to positively identify the deceased, who met with her end by the effects of two gunshot wounds to the head. However, there is a great deal about this case that we do not yet know. The police investigation is continuing, and it should be allowed to do so after which, we will reconvene to take into consideration any new evidence that comes to light."

He looked over his reading glasses to assure himself that the jury had heard and understood everything that he had said. Following that, testimony was taken from Sargent Ramshall and Superintendent Lyle as to the discovery of the body and from Doctor Moxton as to the cause of death. Martha's body had been moved back to the house for positive identification. This was performed by Elizabeth Lister rather than Michael Morrell. He was not called upon at all. The Jury were shown the body, which was on a stretcher laid out in the kitchen, and the obvious points of interest. The broken pane of glass. The footpath outside. Luckily it had stopped snowing and was now visible. Finally, the chair in which she was found murdered.

The jury where then ordered to return to the dining room and Sidney Taylor gave the final address to them.

“As it is Easter Sunday tomorrow, and as I stated earlier, that the Police should have more time to investigate, I will adjourn this hearing until Monday the tenth of April”.

And then it was finished, temporarily. A crowd had gathered outside of Balmoral House, the jury and officials had to navigate their way through them in order to leave. Unnoticed by them in the throng, Keith Smedley was there. He wanted to somehow assure himself that it was all true. That Martha Morrell was dead. Killed, no doubt, with his gun. He thought that William Aitkens would be there too as he was involved in the original raising of the alarm of the murder. But he was not. Keith guessed that he would be at Rockside Hydro. He began to walk in that direction.

Chapter 25: A Ring of Irony

William Aitkens listened patiently to Keith Smedley.

"We have waited too long to trap the mayor and the monster. And now look what has happened? Martha Morrell is dead! Killed by one or the other to prevent us from finding out more about *it*, and them, and their collusion to conceal what is really happening in this town!"

There were words of truth in what was said. William had thought that it was best to take no action until after Easter. The religious holiday was well patronised by all of the Christian faiths in the area. And the Mayor was often involved with the various clergy to lend a hand with readings and collections and charitable works surrounding the celebration.

The door to Aitkens office was closed so that nobody could overhear them. In spite of everything, the Easter celebration could offer them an opportunity rather than a barrier. William pondered briefly and offered his revised plan.

"I propose that we reiterate the same scheme that saw you duped at the Wesleyan Chapel but add our own twist to it. Make it seem more real and urgent"

This did not give enough away of the plan for Smedley to comment either way. He just shook his head indicating that he needed more information. William continued.

"Instead of luring the Mayor to a trap with the promise of information about the strange goings on in Matlock, threaten him with exposure; under the guise of extorting money from him. Here is what I am thinking. The Mayor, if he really is involved and is guilty, will sacrifice all of his normal Easter duties in order to make the meeting. The entire town will be distracted by the Easter services. It will be a perfect cover. Write him a note, or rather, I will write him a note, I am left handed you are right handed, the slope of the writing will be different enough to ensure that he doesn't suspect that it is you."

William paused for a breath and then went into more detail.

"Ask for a sum of money to ensure that it will be taken seriously. Say that you saw him approaching and leaving Balmoral house on the night of Martha's murder and you will go to the police and give testimony unless he pays you quite a princely amount."

William waited for Keith's reaction. When the plan had sunk-in, Keith thought that it would be perfect.

"If he is the one that did it, he will want to meet the person and perhaps kill them too. If it was the monster that did it, he will still want to meet the person and get rid of them for the sake of his accomplice. I think that is brilliant William. We should do it."

Both men knew that reusing the same ploy that the Mayor used to lure Smedley to his planned death, had a nice ring of irony to it.

“You must consider the possibility of failure though, please keep that in mind” warned William. Keith knew what he was referring too, but put it into words anyway.

“If the Mayor isn’t involved at all, he will take the note to the Police…..How will we know?”

It was a quandary with a simple solution.

“I’ll have one of my men watch the Mayor’s Office when we know that the note has been delivered. If he comes storming out and makes his way to the Police or even sends for them, then we will know that we are wrong.” William looked to Keith for acceptance of the measure that he would put in place. Keith agreed.

“The next thing that we should do is choose a place to meet the Mayor, or the monster; somewhere that will not immediately point to our involvement. But somewhere out of sight enough for him to warrant it a safe place to meet an extortionist”. William left the question opened ended.

Both men came up with various places, but each time it was deemed to be not quite right for one reason or another. They we are running out of ideas when William came up with a suggestion.

“How about a place outside of Matlock, down at Matlock Bath for example?” Keith liked the idea. The first place that came to mind was Mary Whittaker’s establishment that fed all of the hydro businesses in Matlock.

“The Matlock Bath Mineral Water Works. Mary is a confident of mine. I am sure that I could convince her to come onboard.” Keith embraced the idea enthusiastically.

“If you can do that, then we have ourselves a plan that will work. I will draught three of my best men, along with you and I, that will be more than enough” William’s face showed that the plan had come together nicely. There was one thing that needed to be accounted for though.

“He will have my gun for sure” reminded Keith.

“We will have four, safety in numbers and all that you know” smiled William.

It was set. William then busied himself writing the note. It was brief.

I saw you approach and leave Balmoral House on the night of Martha Morrell’s murder. Unless you pay me the sum of £200, I will tell the Police what I saw. Bring the money to the Mineral Water Works in Matlock Bath on Easter Sunday at noon.

They studied the letter together. It met with both of their approvals. Keith was surprised at the amount of money being sought.

“Two hundred pounds. A year’s wage for a professional man” he observed.

“I’m sure that Thaddeus Tremorlund has more than that secreted around is house. Besides, he won’t bring any money with him. He will be solely concerned with silencing anyone that can implicate him in the murder of Martha Morrell."

William was being pragmatic. One last thought occurred to Keith.

"What will you tell your men?" he inquired.

"Leave that to me; it's all in hand already" William answered rather mysteriously. Keith decided not to push the matter. It was more than enough that the mayor was about to become trapped in a web of retribution.

"Get Mary Whittaker's approval to use her establishment. And then we will deliver the note to the City Hall. There is never a day of the week that Thaddeus is not there for some amount of time. I'll post my man to watch the goings on and let you know how it all unfolds." William was becoming caught up in the moment. It was all going in exactly the direction that Keith wanted. Soon the Mayor and his accomplice would be laid bare before credible witnesses. He would have absolutely nowhere to hide.

***

Mary Whittaker was surprisingly easy to convince. More so than Keith would have thought. She either saw that Keith was desperate for exoneration with his views or that it would help seal the fact that it was all imagined. It seemed to Keith that either way Mary looked at the situation, there would be a resolution one way or the other. Keith dutifully reported back to William who dispatched his man to both surreptitiously deliver the note and then watch for the reaction from the Mayor.

***

It was easy for James Green of the Rockside Hydro to blend in with the people coming and going in the town hall. Luckily as it was Easter Saturday, there were fewer than normal. He saw an opportunity and secreted himself into the hallway. After observing that the Mayor was not in his office, he waited for an absence of people and slipped the envelope beneath the door.

All that he knew was that nobody should see him deliver the note, and above all watch for the Mayor's reaction. He will either go directly to the police or directly home to agonise about its contents. It wasn't up to James to know exactly what was going on, but it was exciting to be involved. The young man of only 28 years of age was walking down the corridor when he saw the Mayor approach from the outside steps. He quickly plonked himself down and picked up a newspaper that was on a table opening it up to cover his face.

Unsurprisingly the Mayor paid absolutely no attention to the person sitting in the hallway reading a paper. It was a common enough sight. If he had thought that maybe it was something that he would see more often during the week rather than on a Saturday, Easter Saturday no less, then he may have been suspicious. But it did not occur to him.

Opening his office door, the envelope was immediately noticeable against the dark green carpet. James watched over the paper as the Mayor bent down with a harrumph and righted himself to open the envelope and study the contents. Luckily more people had come in behind the mayor, three in all and were discussing something petty, nearby. They offered ready-made additional cover for James.

The Mayor visibly tensed upon reading the note. He exited his office slamming the door. With a look of panic on his face he hurriedly made his exit, once more not taking in anyone or anything happening in the hallway. James put down his paper and followed the Mayor to the front door. He remained behind and watched the Mayor descend the outside stone stairs in a undignified manner before turning left. This was the direction that he would take if he was returning to his home. If he had turned right, then it would be a sure sign that he was heading for the Police Station.

James's mission was accomplished. He remained at the door looking out of the glass long enough to reassure himself that the Mayor was indeed going directly home. There was nothing further for him to do. He looked around him. Nobody was paying him the slightest attention. Time to report back to his employer, Mister William Aitkens that all had gone exactly as he was told.

Chapter 26: Easter Sunday 2nd April 1893

Easter Sunday had a more sombre note to it in the light of the cold-blooded murder of Martha Morrell. It was the only subject of conversation on everybody's lips. The Mayor was conspicuous by his absence from all of the major religious services. It certainly wasn't like him to miss the opportunity to show his face to the constituents. He would normally flit from one to the other, but not this time.

Nevertheless, the majority of the religious celebrations were held at noon on Easter Sunday. Matlock was for all intents and purposes a ghost-town. Anybody who was anybody was at a mass, or service or the like. And being the Easter celebration, they were due to run for much longer than usual, followed by gatherings in various church halls and grounds.

Snow had given way to rain. It was raining, and nobody wanted to be outside. It was cosier to be inside with the various congregations involved in the Easter celebrations.

If Matlock was all but deserted, then Matlock Bath to its south was positively barren of people. The Matlock Bath Mineral Water Works was a structure built upon a naturally occurring rift in the rock surrounding the river Derwent that snaked through both Matlock and Matlock Bath. On the side of the river where the Mineral Water Works sat, it was hard rock. Beneath that, a reservoir of mineral waters, that bizarrely did not mix with, or become contaminated by the river water that ran past it by only a few feet.

The discovery in the middle of the century, had led to the rise of the hydro business enterprises of Matlock and the surrounding towns. Those hydro businesses that were situated in places where they could not drive down their own bore and extract the health-giving mineral waters, relied upon the Mineral Water Works to supply them with the desired commodity.

Keith Smedley, William Aitkens, Joseph Rowlett, Henry Bradshaw and James Green had secreted themselves inside the establishment three hours prior to the meeting. It was a necessary safety measure.

The Mayor may elect to come half and hour or an hour earlier to see who approached, but it was guessed that he would not have the tenacity or forethought to think of staking-out the water works from 9am. The monster on the other hand was an unknown quantity.

So as to circumvent any possible observation, each of the men approached the meeting place from a different angle. In that way, there would be no chance of being detected as a group of people descending upon the water works.

They waited inside, barely talking. The cavernous waterworks with its pumping system could have easily hidden any conversation, but the pump was not working today. It caused an eerie silence in the large pumping room. Not one that either Keith or William were accustomed to. They had in fact, never been here before without the machinery in operation. It was quite strange.

Keith noted that getting any lengthy conversation out of the young staff that William had brought with him was difficult anyway. All in their twenties or at most thirty years of age, Keith put it down to nerves. They were here to trap a town conspirator. They all had guns, it must have been quite nerve-racking for the young men.

The hours ticked past uneventfully. Keith and William together, put in place the final pieces of the strategy. There was three ways in which the Mayor could enter the building. Two of them were basically side doors which were bolted shut on the inside by the posse. In this way, the Mayor would be driven to come in by the main door only.

Mary Whittaker was nowhere in sight. Keith didn't think much of it at the time presuming that she was at one of the religious celebrations. It was good of her to allow them to use her establishment in this way.

Time seemed to slow down moving from 11am onwards. The men were positioned at various points that overlooked the main pumping room and its entry. They needed to basically surround anyone who came in, but not be visible until ordered.

The final piece of the puzzle was William Aitkens. When the Mayor showed up, it would be him that would confront the man. That way it would look like a real attempt at blackmail. Showing Keith's face would immediately be recognised as a trap of some description.

Fifteen minutes to go. Aitkens men were already deployed and out of sight. Keith would be the one that prevented escape, he was closest to the entrance, but well hidden behind some enormous pipes, over-engineered and bolted together with more bolts that it would have needed should it operate for a hundred years.

Ten minutes to go and hearts jumped as there was a noise at the door. It was a pigeon that had run into the door and become stunned. Keith gingerly investigated and indicated to the others that it was nothing. They all resumed their assigned places.

Five minutes to go and doubt began to set in to Keith's mind. What if the Mayor and the Monster did not show up? What would they do? How else would they hope to catch them and expose what they have been doing together in the town?

Then, all of a sudden it was noon. There was a clock in the main pump room that chimed twelve times marking the mid-point of the day. Testament to his impeccable civil manners the Mayor tentatively opened the door to the main pump room upon the twelfth chime.

He walked in looking for all the world like he expected somebody to pounce upon him at any second. There was a gantry in front of him, it led to the middle of the room and overlooked the main bore and pump. He proceeded toward the half-way point and stopped.

"I'm here; I have what you want" shouted the mayor to the seemingly empty room. His voice echoed in the stillness. He held up an envelope which looked thick with paper, presumably bills.

Keith was unsure of why William hesitated, perhaps it was for dramatic effect, perhaps he was having second thoughts; but eventually he stood up from his hiding point. He was on another gantry higher and to the right of the room. He looked at what appeared to be the quivering Mayor.

"Thaddeus; how are you?" asked William in what appeared to be quite a snide tone. Excellent, work thought Keith, exactly how a blackmailer would act.

"William Aitkens? I don't believe it! You? What would you want with two-hundred pounds? You must make that amount every month in your business?" Thaddeus was clearly disconcerted.

"Did I forget to tell you that I would be requiring the same amount on the anniversary of what I saw, to ensure that the police never find out about you being at Balmoral House when Martha Morrell was murdered."

William was playing the part perfectly. He could have been a Shakespearian actor on a stage; he was absolutely convincing. The Mayor's reaction was exactly as expected.

"What? That's outrageous! Who do you think you are holding me to ransom?" he said, agitated and angry.

"Let's not talk about the future Thaddeus. Let's concentrate upon the present, shall we? I believe the contents of that envelope are for me? Why don't you wait right there, and I will come down to collect it?"

William had to turn around to safely descend the ladder connecting the two disparate levels of gantries. He was exposed. If the Mayor produced a gun, Keith's gun, he would be done for. Keith tensed, but the mayor made no such move.

William was on an intersecting gantry now, on the same level as Thaddeus. They regarded each other from afar. They both looked like they were sizing each other up for a fight. But in reality, the Mayor was a much older man, he wouldn't have stood a chance.

William began to walk slowly and deliberately toward the Mayor. They never took their eyes off one another. William rounded a corner and was now on the section of gantry where Thaddeus stood. He began the short walk to the middle of the gantry to join him.

"I'd like to thank you for this Thaddeus. You've been very cooperative. And I hope that you continue to be so" William said to him, not really expecting an answer. However, the Mayor's tone changed dramatically. No longer was he the hunted in this battle of wits.

"No William, I would like to thank *you* for arranging this meeting. I simply had to know who it was that saw me arrive and leave Balmoral House the other night. I should have suspected that it was one of the neighbours. And after all, Rockside is close enough to be a neighbour. Where were you exactly when you saw me?"

Thaddeus was level-headed and quite brazen. William's eyes narrowed; the sudden altering of attitude was cause for concern. He continued to walk toward Thaddeus and stopped about two feet away from him.

"Does it matter? All you need to be concerned with is that should I offer testimony of what was witnessed, you will be in a very awkward position indeed."

William was still playing the game. He had not admitted to the ruse yet.

"Standing in front of me as you are William, you will find that it is you who are in an untenable position, not I". Thaddeus smiled snidely.

"Meaning, what exactly?" demanded William.

At that point the door opened, and a man entered. Keith recognised him immediately. He took in a sharp intake of breath and prayed that nobody heard it. He gingerly repositioned himself to take in the scene but still without revealing himself. Keith's heart began to race.

"Who is this?" asked William looking daggers at the newcomer.

"Allow me to introduce myself" said the newcomer "Captain Benjamin Brigges; at your service" he said.

As he spoke he lifted a gun from his side and pointed it directly at William's head. Keith recognised it immediately. It was his gun. The one that would have been used to murder Martha Morrell. The one that could easily incriminate him in the murder investigation undertaken by the authorities.

To his credit, William had a much more low-key response than would have been expected under the circumstances.

"Pleased to make your acquaintance Captain Brigges, my name is William Aitkens, proprietor of the Rockside Hydropathic establishment on Cavendish road. If you'll excuse us, Mayor Tremorlund and I have business to take care of, and pointing a gun at my head is distracting me, as you can imagine." William managed a wry smile.

The absurdity of the instruction was not lost on either the Mayor or the Captain. They both looked at each other and burst out in raucous laughter. Brigges laughter however, was more malicious in tone. The evilness could be heard in it with remarkable clarity. When they had both settled down it was Brigges who pointed out the precarious position that William appeared to be in.

"I don't think that you are in a position to dictate terms Mister Aitkens. After all, I am the one holding the gun." He waved it about gently to assure that William noticed the weapon.

Mayor Tremorlund took up the teasing. He held up the envelope and then opened it. He removed the contents. It was newspaper cut into sections that resembled the dimensions of currency.

"And I have no intention of being blackmailed today, or at any time in the future William!" He said. As he concluded his taunt, he flung the papers off the gantry and they fluttered downwards dispersing themselves as they fell.

William looked over the edge of the gantry at the falling papers. He righted himself and admonished both men.

“Mary is not going to be happy at you making a mess of her pumping station gentlemen! I suggest that you make good the error of your ways and clean up the mess that you’ve made”

William sounded for all the world like he was dead-serious. This provoked another round of laughter from the pair. When it had subsided, it was Brigges that answered.

“The only *cleaning up* that will be done here today Mister Aitkens will be when I devour you. My associate may have to dispose of what is left. But I am quite hungry, having not fed since the matlockite miners, so he may not even have to do that!”

Brigges had lost his glib tone; he was dead-serious. His eyes shone with lust; the desire to feast once more upon a human body.

Chapter 27: The Trap

William should have looked more alarmed than he did; it irked Brigges. Instead of being horrified, Aitkens instead lifted both of his arms in what appeared to be either a surrender, or a prayer to the Almighty, above. His action could have been taken both ways. Unknown to Brigges and Tremorlund however, was that this action was the predetermined signal for his hidden accomplices, to show themselves.

In unison, Joseph, Henry, James and Keith all revealed their positions. Each was pointing a hand gun at the pair of miscreants. Thaddeus jumped with surprise. His face showing absolute panic.

"What is this?!" he shouted; the situation had turned around so dramatically it was difficult for him to comprehend. He looked like a cornered animal looking desperately for a way to escape.

Brigges let out an inhuman growl verbalising his displeasure at the turn of events. Aitkens allowed the scene to be taken in by Brigges and Tremorlund before stating the very obvious.

"We have you surrounded, there is absolutely no hope of escape, and I think that even you'll agree Captain Brigges that you could not survive being shot by four guns. All nicely in range and aimed at the ringleader of the events that have unsettled so many people here in quiet little Matlock and the surrounding towns."

Aitkens waited for a reaction of some kind, but received none. Thaddeus was too paralysed with fear to do anything and Brigges was looking from one to the other as if trying to assess and reassess is predicament over and over. William continued.

"Hand over the gun Captain Benjamin Brigges and I assure you that this situation will be resolved quickly and to everyone's satisfaction".

Williams words echoed though the cavernous building. Brigges, however did not look like he was going to readily give up the pistol that he was aiming at Aitkens. Thaddeus was beginning to panic. He began to blather.

"Do as he says Brigges, for pity's sake! We are surrounded" Thaddeus's voice was quivering with fear. Brigges did not take kindly to the thought of giving up so easily. It could be seen in his eyes that he indented to go down fighting.

His eyes narrowed, and he pulled the trigger of the gun he was holding, releasing a bullet directly at William Aitkens. It was all over in an instant of a second.

The bullet impacted William in the centre of his chest. He lurched backwards but miraculously did not fall over. He righted himself and once more held up both hands in a gesture to his consorts.

"Don't fire!" he commanded.

Keith was absolutely stunned. William should have been dead, but instead was standing, facing his assailant with a look of irritation on his face.

"No more shooting Captain Brigges. Surely you realise that it will take more than bullets to dispose of *people* like you and me?"

Aitkens was uninjured, but Keith and Thaddeus couldn't for the life of them understand how he had survived a near point-blank shot to the chest. And then there was the reference to 'people like you and me', what was that supposed to mean? Keith looked around at the younger men. They all had completely failed to react in the same way that he and the Mayor were doing. What was going on? Couldn't they see the inexplicable situation unfolding before them?

Keith and Thaddeus managed to make eye contact in the ensuing moments. It was clear that they were the only two that appeared to be amazed at what was unfolding.

Aitkens and Brigges were staring at each other in a way that was hard to define. It wasn't anger, nor was it curiosity, nor was it any of the human emotions that should have been associated with what was happening.

Thaddeus and Keith simultaneously noticed that William's face had begun to glow in a strange fashion. Thaddeus had seen in before, when Captain Brigges changed his form during the hot air balloon ride. It was happening again, only this time it was William Aitkens that was losing his facial features.

They blurred and dissolved into nothing. There was no mouth anymore. No eyes or nose; all that was left was a jelly-like surface that replaced what should have been William's face. Then, just as quickly as it happened, it was reversed. The smiling face of William Aitkens was once more in place exactly where it had been moments before.

It all happened so quickly that Keith began to immediately doubt if he had actually seen what he witnessed. His heart was racing, he didn't know what to do. Again, he looked to Joseph, James and Henry; the had failed to react at all. In fact, now that he was looking at them again, he could see that they had blank expressions on their face, like they were cleverly made wax-mannequin facsimiles of the young men that he knew.

Thaddeus had narrowed his eyes and looked more carefully at William, then back to Brigges and returning his gaze to Aitkens once more. He spoke, his voice quivering with fear.

"You're one of those; one of them? One of him; like him!" he said, his blathering somehow making sense, as he pointed at Brigges.

"I am indeed" confirmed William smiling politely at Thaddeus as if absolutely nothing was out of the ordinary.

"Now Captain Brigges, once more; please hand me that gun, no good will come of using it. Hand-it to Thaddeus and he can pass it across to me." William instructed.

Brigges hesitated and looked around him again his eyes stopping upon Keith. There was a naked flash of anger; it was unmistakable. Keith's breath became short; but he tried his best not to show any fear in the face of such evil.

It looked as if Brigges was not going to comply. In fact, if he had laid money on it, Keith would have guessed that rather than surrender his firearm, Brigges would have preferred to use it on him. The tension in the air was thick. Keith looked around him once more. It seemed for all the world like his compatriots would not be able to save him if Brigges took aim and fired. There was nothing for it, he would simply have to fire first.

Keith stretched out his arm, he was shaking. At this distance any shot fired may well miss the mark completely; but he simply had to try. What else could he do?

"Very well" conceded Brigges, diffusing the situation that had arisen to his side.

Keith let out an audible breath of relief. Brigges turned the gun around and taking the barrel, he pushed the handle toward the Mayor. Thaddeus took hold of the gun. He was so nervous that it could be seen to shake quite a lot. He repeated the action and took the barrel and offered the handle of the gun to William.

William relieved Thaddeus of the weapon. The tension in the air eased considerably. It must have been too much for Thaddeus because he began to confess to everything that had led him to this point.

"It was me! I was the one that pushed Albert Brawnly off the walking path at the cliff. I didn't want some drunkard idiot raising the spectre of a monster haunting Matlock; it would have been disastrous for our town, for our economy, for our standing in Derbyshire! You must see that surely?"

William and Brigges did not react at all to Thaddeus's confession. Nor did the young men in William's employ. Keith however, was horrified. His mouth dropped open, he wanted to admonish the mayor for his callousness and murderous ways, but no words came out.

As if taking the abject silence as permission to continue, he let them know of his next deed.

"And the miners too, when I found them slaughtered in the mine, I couldn't let it be known that there was a savage beast amongst us. It would have been mayhem. There was no outcome that I could see that would have been good for anyone, anyone at all. People could have abandoned our town in droves for fear of their own lives. People could have come from miles around looking for the creature? My perfect little town was going to be ruined either way. I had to make it look like an accident. And the dynamite was right there. It was providence. Yes; that's what it was! It was meant to be covered up by someone like me, that cares, really cares about what happens to Matlock. You can see that can't you?"

The Mayor was close to tears. He really believed that the evil that he had done was in the best interests of everyone. He was so self-deluded, that he thought that he could convince the people surrounding him of it too.

Keith interjected at this point. He was so astounded at the revelations coming from the Mayor that he wanted to know about the one that was most important to him.

“And Martha? Was it in everybody’s best interests that she die, as well?” He was angry, and it showed. However, it was Brigges that entered the fray here.

“That Witch could summon the dead. She had to be silenced. I couldn’t risk being exposed now that I have decided to settle-down here in Matlock. So, I sent my willing accomplice to finish her off once and for all! And, he did such a good job. Didn’t you Thaddeus?” Brigges smirked vindictively.

Thaddeus actually looked ashamed now. He was uncertain how to answer. He stammered and tried his best to compose himself.

“I did as I was told!” he managed to say, wiping away a tear.

“So, it *was* you”

Keith’s words seemed to pierce the heart of Thaddeus as they were spoken.

“A harmless little old lady, living a quiet life in the hills of Derbyshire, and you *shot* her!” Keith was sickened. The Mayor tried his best to stifle his crying, unsuccessfully. He was ashamed of his actions.

“Be kind mister Smedley” said the creature, turning to face him.

“What else could he do? If he hadn’t killed the old-hag, then I would have simply done it myself and devoured him for being so non-compliant. And, the gun that you supplied so stupidly was the perfect weapon. I simply couldn’t lose any way that you looked at it. The police would have eventually *found* the gun, and I was going to ensure that you were implicated in some way.”

Keith jumped in at this point to defend himself.

“But I had an alibi; people saw me at Smedley’s at the time of the murder, it couldn’t possibly have been me!” he said.

Brigges shook his head as if admonishing a school boy.

“Any implication in the murder will have served me Mister Smedley. You had an alibi; so what? You were the one attempting to raise the alarm about my presence. Any chance to throw doubt on you would have worked in my favour. Give me some credit, I am usually very inventive with the people that I play my games with. And you had so irritatingly eluded the *accidental* death that I had planned for you, that I had to do something else to silence you. Clever of me don’t you think?’

Brigges was actually asking for praise from Smedley, it turned Keith’s stomach. A good woman had died as part of his spiteful plan. Keith was almost unable to grasp the kind of wickedness that was intrinsic to this creature.

William Aitkens signalled to his three men to approach. They did so without speaking. Keith’s sense of revulsion with the creature was giving way to satisfaction. Now this unspeakable abomination was going to get what was coming to it. He began to speculate on what would become of the thing. Maybe it would be dissected to see what makes it tick. Something the scientists all around the country would be sure to want to do. Maybe it would be put into a travelling freak show to terrify onlookers for a fee. A humiliating punishment for the beast, but one that was sitting quite well with Keith Smedley. Keith had managed to block temporarily from his memory what he had seen. William was one of these creatures too. A kind of willing temporary amnesia enveloped Keith. He had deliberately forgotten that William Aitkens was the same as Benjamin Brigges, a creature that defied description.

He kept imagining all sorts of bad outcomes for the captured monster when the most incredible thing happened. William handed Keith's gun over to Joseph and then spoke to them.

"Return to Rockside, remove the sentinels from the backs of your neck and place them in on my desk. Oh, and take this back to Rockside with you as well."

Nothing of what he said made any sense to Keith, it may as well have been in another language completely.

"What are you doing?" he said incredulously. They were victorious, and he was handing away that advantage. William looked earnestly at Keith and answered.

"Somebody could get hurt with all of these guns around Keith. There's a good chap Joseph, Henry, James be on your way now."

It was uninterpretable enough for William to ask for his posse to leave the scene at the point of victory, but even more amazing when the three men appeared to be complying without any argument whatsoever. They didn't seem phased at all that their employer was of the same ilk as the thing that they had so effectively trapped. Brigges spoke before they had a chance to leave.

"Sentinels?" he asked.

William obligingly stopped the nearest young man to him and turned him around. He pulled down his collar revealing what looked to be a small black sea urchin of some kind stuck into the back of his neck. It had been hidden by the collar of his coat and shirt. But it must have been there the entire time.

"What is it?" asked Keith still unsure of what was going on around him.

"It's a small creature that we can expel at force. It renders the recipient very susceptible to suggestion. In short, it makes them very compliant to what I tell them to do. When they return to Rockside and remove them, it will take a few minutes and their independence will return, but they will not remember much of what has happened to them. I'll tell them that they had a whisky drinking competition and passed out for a few hours."

"You are like him; a monster and you are going to terrorise this town together in cahoots!" Keith accused William of the ultimate sadistic conspiracy.

"Good heavens no!" hollered William with genuine horror.

“I may be like Brigges, or whatever your real name is, but I have absolutely no intention of allowing him to run rampant in our quiet little town. That is completely out of the question.”

Keith and Thaddeus watched in amazement as the three employees of William Aitkens left the pumping station. Keith left his vantage point still brandishing his gun and approached Brigges. He stopped close enough so as to ensure that if he did fire, he would be assured to hit his target. As the young men left, Mary Whittaker entered. She barely acknowledged the youngsters as they left passed her. As she entered onto the main gantry it was as if she was taking a Sunday afternoon stroll. The rain had started to fall heavily again. It could be heard impacting the roof and windows of the building.

Keith reacted chivalrously and begged her to leave.

“No Mary, please this is the monster of Matlock, get out of here as quickly as you can, and get the police, for pities sake!” he was beginning to become frantic under the indescribable circumstances.

For her part Mary only smiled politely at Keith as if she hadn’t believed a word that came out of his mouth.

“Hello Mary” said William greeting the lady as she approached.

“My Dear William, you appear to have captured the troublemaker that has upset our quiet little town.” She gave a distasteful look at Brigges as she walked up to them.

There they stood the five of them; Thaddeus and Keith looked absolutely perplexed, Mary and William with knowing looks being passed to each other and Brigges looked suspiciously at his former captor.

The penny dropped for Thaddeus first.

"You; you're one of them too!" he said accusingly and rudely pointing at Mary.

"Of course, I am Thaddeus. And it's rude to point. One would think a man in your position would have more refined manners than that?" she admonished the Mayor.

Keith's entire world was collapsing around him. He didn't know what to think anymore. William Aitkens, Mary Whittaker were the same as Benjamin Brigges, some kind of unspeakable horror. Would they bandy together, or what? He didn't know what to do, what to think. He was incapable of processing the information that he was receiving.

"What are you? What are the three of you? What are you?!" he screamed at them clutching his head with his hands.

William and Mary gave Keith a look of worry. As if they were concerned for his state of being.

"Please calm yourself Mister Smedley" begged Mary.

"We have no intention of allowing this miscreant to go on terrorising our little township, do we Mary?" said William reassuringly.

"Of course not; it will never do. Must be stopped at once" she said complying with William's sentiments.

None of this was lifting the veil of confusion that Keith and Thaddeus were feeling. Brigges for his part was becoming increasingly agitated.

“Did I hear you correctly earlier; I was listening from behind the door. Terribly rude of me but necessary under the circumstances. Captain of the Mary Celeste?” Mary looked inquisitively at Brigges for a reply.

“Yes; what of it?” he asked in annoyance.

“A merchant ship found adrift off the Azores some years back. Passengers and crew missing without a trace. Your handiwork I take it?” she had an accusatory tone to her question. Brigges mood was darkening with each passing second.

“I enjoyed my time aboard the Mary Celeste, it was very amusing to watch them grapple with one death after the other, unsure of what was really happening to them.”

Brigges was revelling in telling others about his unspeakable acts of horror. But Mary and William did not rise to the occasion. They gave Brigges looks of absolute disgust. Brigges was angry at the high-handed attitude of his fellow creatures.

“Surely you do the same; if you are really like me?” He looked from one to the other, to his front and back for some sort of affirmation that they too were like him, a sadistic monster that took pleasure in the misery of others. But he was disappointed.

“I can tell you in all honesty Captain Brigges that Keith and I are nothing like you whatsoever”

As she spoke she gave him a condescending shake of her head, looking down her nose at him. This infuriated Brigges.

“You must be if you are like me. It’s what we do. It’s how I amuse myself before I absorb somebody and take over their life, like you must have done the both of you to have those human-shaped bodies.” He pointed violently at William as he shouted at them. Mary replied to Brigges.

“The real Mary Whittaker was nearly dead with cancer of the throat when I found her. I offered to relieve her of her suffering, and perpetuate her life by proposing absorption. I effectively took over the life that she was about to lose anyway. To her friends and family, it was a miracle. She had miraculously recovered from the unrecoverable. In the end, Mary was grateful to me for ending her suffering and sparing her loved ones the agony of losing somebody dear to them. It was a perfectly reciprocal arrangement; agreed to by both parties.”

Mary was genuine. She looked to William nodding that he should tell his story to the small group.

“William Aitkens drowned whilst on holiday. I found him only moments after death had already taken him. I absorbed his body and became William Aitkens. He returned from his evening swim to his family and friends as if nothing had ever happened. Imagine their horror if they had found that he had drowned whilst holidaying with them. Fortunately for me, he was a very savvy business man. A man of quite some wealth. I used his money and invested it wisely in the Rockside Hydrotherapy Establishment which has been a great success. Testament to his business acumen. I am grateful to him for everything that I have gained from William Aitkens. I will never be able to thank him. But I can live a life for him that was forfeit; surely a noble sentiment?"

Keith looked to Thaddeus and Keith and then Brigges. Each had vastly different reactions to the two amazing stories that they had just heard.

Keith was dumbfounded. He thought that on the surface it sounded honourable, but couldn't reconcile the fact that the people that he thought he knew were really something else entirely.

Thaddeus was trying to work out how he could turn this information around to something that would assist him get out of this situation altogether. You could see it in his face, his mind was working furiously.

Brigges however was becoming more incensed with every passing second. He was being admonished by his peers. Ones that until now he didn't even know existed.

"I thought that I was the only one!" he spat at them vehemently.

"The only sentient Siphonophore? No, no, no Benjamin. We are a new lifeform emerging from the sea. But because of that we need to be careful. We have a need to integrate with human society and live peacefully within it. That is what we do. We certainly don't lurk in the shadows. Nor do we murder the entire crew of a boat for pleasure!" If Mary was condescending before she was positively patronising now. It did not sit will with Brigges at all who emitted a low growl of displeasure directed straight at her.

Keith wasn't sure where to look. He was so taken aback with the events and what he had learned. He thought that he knew the world around him but all of that was in doubt. Here was a secret new lifeform living amongst them that nobody else had ever heard of. He scratched his head. Suddenly there was another person standing with them. It was a woman. He recognised her immediately from the séance that he attended overseen by Martha Morrell. He spoke aloud.

"Elizabeth Stride"

They all looked at him. Keith was staring at where she had stood only a second ago, but she was now gone. An apparition that appeared, just like Alice Athalia had done on the tram, effectively giving him a way to distract the creature and save his life. This had a similar effect. Although Mary, Thaddeus and William had no idea who Elizabeth Stride was or how she figured into this conversation, Brigges recognized the name immediately.

"One of my tastier victims, in London a few years ago; what of her?" he said looking daggers at Smedley. William reacted though.

"I know that name, it was in all of the papers for ages a few years back." William tried to remember then put his finger on it.

"Jack the Ripper? You were Jack the Ripper? I don't believe it! You are out of control Brigges, you have to be stopped here and now!" the threat hung in the air like a dank smell.

Brigges growled again, only this time directed at Aitkens.

"How else do you gain sustenance except by absorbing one of these insignificant things and taking their form over and over?" Brigges was angry, he spat the words at Mary and William.

"You silly thing" admonished Mary.

"No wonder you are in such a mess. You have been taking form after form, don't you know that it is part of our way to take and hold a form for as many years, decades as we can before moving on to another human identity. Altering our form is not a cheap trick for the sake of a temporary disguise. It will cause all sorts of problems. And I am sure that it already has." Keith looked keenly into Brigges eyes.

"Are you having trouble holding a human form?" he asked.

Brigges seemed to become uncomfortable immediately. He looked down unable to hold Keith's penetrating gaze.

"I can see that you do" observed Keith. He continued

"Is this form of Captain Brigges the one that you can hold for the longest? Without reverting to your true shape?"

Brigges nodded almost imperceptibly, as if ashamed of his secret being discovered and laid bare before them.

"Not surprising" quipped Mary "It must have been one of the bodies that you emulated earlier on in your life, before you started to come asunder by transforming too often. This is really all your own fault Captain Brigges. Our abilities are meant to help integrate us with high society here on land; it is not a cheap parlour trick to fool the unwary." Her annoyance with Brigges was plain to see. Then she had a sudden thought and turned her attentions to Thaddeus.

"I still don't understand his hold over *you* Mayor Tremorlund. Was he threatening to devour you if you gave away his identity?"

Thaddeus almost jumped. He was unprepared for the question and he mumbled and fumbled his way through a number of half answers before finally coming completely clean.

"There was a payment, three rings that were promised if I helped him. Huge diamonds, the largest that I have ever seen; Tiffany was quite taken with them too." Thaddeus looked at Brigges as if he was expecting the monster to produce them here and now. For his part, Brigges glared murderously back at Thaddeus. Mary continued.

"You may still have them Thaddeus. I know where within his……*our* physiology, he will be storing them; a kind of sack about where a human spleen would be. We can recover them from his body for you. Join us!"

Mary's words electrified the room like a bolt of lightning. The tables had turned again. The unexpected offer of payment for the Mayor to effectively change sides was the reassurance that Keith Smedley needed to comfort himself that the situation was still under control.

Brigges looked for all the world like he was about to murder the Mayor where he stood for even contemplating the offer. Thaddeus instinctively moved away from Brigges and toward Aitkens.

"Don't you even think about it you worthless parasite!"

Brigges insult was warning the Mayor to not take up the offer. But Thaddeus was nothing if not pragmatic. He was a politician after all, albeit local government. The tide had turned, and he was more than prepared to go with the flow in this instance. Besides, it would serve him in the long term, and gain his expected reward anyway. Tiffany would be pleased he thought.

Seeing the growing hostility from Brigges, Keith Smedley stepped forward brandishing the gun reminding the monster that he was still in his sights. Brigges ignored the threat and looked as if he was still planning to pounce on Thaddeus and take his revenge on the traitor right here and now.

"Please put that gun away Keith" begged William. "If you fire it, it will more than likely do either yourself of Thaddeus more harm than it will for one of our kind. We are quite resilient when it comes to firearms."

William Aitkens and Mary Whittaker looked at Keith Smedley as if expecting him to comply with this quite obvious directive. But he hesitated.

"Give up our advantage?" he said sceptically.

"That gun is no advantage against a sentient Siphonophore Keith. Please just put it away. If you don't believe me then fire.

Straight at Brigges, aim for the middle of the eyes and see what happens?" Mary stood back holding her hands in the pose of an annoyed headmistress dressing-down a naughty pupil.

There was a stalemate. Keith was unwilling to allow Brigges out of his sights, but if what Mary had said was true, there was no point to him aiming the gun at his prisoner in the first place. It was Brigges who either connivingly or unwittingly confirmed the reality of the situation.

"Yes, Mister Smedley, fire, by all means! Right through me and at that cowering defector!"

Brigges made as if to wrest Mayor Tremorlund toward him. William countered by stepping in his way. Brigges, although furious, was unwilling to take on one of his own kind. He thought the better of his little ruse and backed down.

There was silence. Keith looked to Thaddeus and then down at his gun. It must be true he thought, if guns were a threat to this monster, to these monsters, then William wouldn't have sent is men away with them. He reluctantly lowered his arm.

"That's better" said Mary, pleased with his decision.

"What now?"

Keith spoke as he put the weapon in his jacket pocket. It was the question on Brigges mind as well. William answered.

"The two of us are more than a match for this poor old thing. Exhausted from overuse of his transformational abilities. I would go further to say that when you eat, it is not providing the usual sustenance for you either is it?"

Brigges began to look like a trapped animal. Mary at his back, William at his front. Both of them, threatening.

"No" he admitted. "No matter what I eat, it is not giving me the usual feeling of satisfaction. It is not allowing me to take on new forms, or even hold this one for longer periods, as it used to do."

Maybe it was a play for sympathy from his own kind, but it did not work.

"Unfortunately, you have to die Captain Benjamin Brigges. But, as you've never before come across any of your own species, you may be unaware of how we will relieve you of your suffering. Take solace, it will be quick and as painless as we can manage. There are more of us than you realise, and we have made a good life for ourselves here in Matlock and Matlock Bath. You are a threat to that idyllic life Brigges. You cannot be allowed to terrorise the people of our town. I'm sorry that it has to be this way."

William's words transfixed Brigges. A trial had occurred, and Brigges had just been found guilty by a panel of two of his peers. The sentence was pronounced and looked to be carried out immediately. He was about to die at the hands of these two Siphonophores in a way that he could only speculate about. Brigges put his hands up to his face and let out a loud cry as if he was in pain.

"I'm losing my hold over this body" he said to his fellow creatures. Thaddeus instinctively backed away even further. Mary and William were dubious. It may have been a ruse of some description. But equally it may very well have been true. Keith could see on their faces that they were undecided which.

As they watched, Brigges features dissolved away, as did his clothing. In a matter of seconds, he was nothing more than a quivering mound of jelly roughly the size and shape of the human that had stood there before. Then the form of being tall and thin collapsed. The jelly became less viscous and began to dissolve into a mound before them.

Then without warning it sprang up and stretched itself into a thin column rising above them all and aimed at the main door to the pump room. It shot over and past Mary and Keith and pulled the remainder of itself away in the process. The column of jelly hit the door and splattered into it, reforming in an instant to the shape of Captain Brigges once more. Without looking back, he flung the doors open and ran through them making good his miraculous escape. The monster of Matlock was once more on the loose.

Chapter 28: The Chase

"After him!"

William pointed at the door. It was an order for them all to follow.

"We can't let him get away" shouted Mary as they all began their pursuit of the monster. Thaddeus and Keith couldn't help but oblige. They all wanted to see this creature stopped.

They raced through the door and into the corridor. The main door to the outside was already swinging closed as they entered. They ran after their quarry. Outside the rain was pelting down. It would have normally given them pause for thought about going out in such a downpour, but none of them even hesitated, running down the pathway after Brigges.

The Captain was surprisingly agile for something that both Mary and William had described as a 'poor old thing'. And Brigges may have been gaining more energy from his recent meals than he had admitted to. He was fast, and getting away from them. Or maybe it was the terror that he must have felt having a death-sentence passed upon him from his own kind.

Brigges ran down the pathway and took the right-hand turn toward the river. Keith was astounded. That was surely the wrong way to go? If he had gone the other way he could have headed almost immediately into the forest giving himself the chance of shelter in the driving rain.

As if sensing his thoughts, William shouted to the small group, with Thaddeus straggling behind them.

"If he gets into the river we may lose him, we are more agile in our water-born forms. He has to be stopped!"

Brigges was smarter than he appeared then, thought Smedley. The River had become swollen with the recent melting snow and heavy rainfalls. It was not at risk of bursting its banks, but the swell had come up to the base of the Jubilee Bridge that Brigges was running toward. It crossed the Derwent from what is considered the quiet side of town where the Mineral Water Works was located, to the busy side of town where most of the other businesses lined the high street of North Parade.

They did their best to catch up with him, but Brigges was faster. He ran across the Jubilee Bridge only opened five years before. The ironwork still gleaming with the colours that it had been painted. Brigges stopped half way across. He jumped up on the wrought iron railing and positioned himself between the criss-crossing iron girders that made up the sides of the span.

There must still have been the flair of snide showmanship within him somewhere because he looked at them approaching him, smiled spitefully and waved before hurling himself into the river. Even as his human body flew through the air downwards toward the raging torrent of a river, it was transforming. Keith and Thaddeus may have very well seen the true form of the sentient Siphonophore if they had been closer or could even have understood what they were seeing.

William and Mary reached the point where Brigges left the Jubilee Bridge before Keith and Thaddeus. They stopped and looked at each other in alarm. Keith came up to them and looked over at the fast-flowing water.

"Can you follow him?" he asked.

Mary looked to William as if in silent conversation, discussing the possibility of following Brigges into the water. They leant back from peering over the edge through the iron girders.

"No; we won't, there is no point" William said with the resignation clear in his voice.

"He could be anywhere by now. Look how fast the river is flowing" They had failed in their self-proclaimed role as executioner. Brigges had escaped the justice that would have been metered out to him by his fellow beings.

***

The Captain Benjamin Brigges sentient Siphonophore landed in the swollen river and dived below the raging surface. Even though his tendrils and other sensing protrusions would have been enough to 'see' around him, he had elected to take on a hybrid form and keep his human eyes. He had grown to appreciate the colour and intricate detail that they could perceive. He was not expecting to be able to see much in the muddy river, but he wanted the advantage of having his human eyes available to him anyway.

Immediately that he landed in the water and pulsated his jellyfish-like body to dive below the surface he knew something was very wrong. The water was not flowing fast below the surface at all. He looked up and could see the differential in the surface eddy compared to the unusually still section of water that he had dived into. In fact, the more that he looked around the more unusual it all began to seem. He was in a perfectly clear pocket of water that appeared to be a clear bubble approximately fifty feet long and almost as wide as the river. The muddy flowing currents could be seen above and below and to either side of the still section of water that he was in.

He was not being carried away by the raging torrent as was planned. He swam around a little, quite dazed and confused about how this miraculous enclave of perfectly clear and still water could exist inside the intensely flowing river Derwent. His apprehension began to rise. This was a phenomenon that the had never before encountered. How could it be?

"You murdered me!"

The words flew at Brigges from somewhere behind him, he contorted his gelatinous body to turn around. Madam Alice Athalia was there, floating before him, pointing an accusatory finger. Her hair was floating in the crystalline water. She was absolutely solid, Brigges could tell just from looking at her. Her mouth moved, and he could hear what she was saying. Even though he was not in human form and did not have his human ears. Even though she was underwater and should not have been able to speak, or even breath. Yet there she was pointing a finger and condemning him for his past actions.

“You murdered me; unspeakable thing!” Alice’s face showed her anger. If Brigges had had a heart in his current form it would have been attempting to pound its way out of his chest. He did not, but that did not matter, he was terrified. He contorted himself to swim away from her in the opposite direction. As he did so he almost ran straight into a man. He was tall, old, not as old as Athalia, but Brigges recognised him immediately. It was Benson, Alice Athalia’s butler from her Kensington townhouse in London.

“You murdered me; abomination!” he pointed a crooked finger directly at Brigges. He was angry, very angry. Like Athalia, he was floating in the still water. And in this case blocking his escape from the old woman. It scared Brigges, a lot. If he had had a mouth he would have screamed in fright, but he did not. So, he twisted his body to try once again to make his escape, this time heading directly to the left. This time his pathway was blocked by two people. A young man and woman.

Brigges couldn’t believe what he was seeing. It was junior detective inspector Samuel Gates and his betrothed, Florence Fairclough. They were immaculately attired. They looked for all the world like they were going out to a fancy restaurant in one of the more affluent areas of London. Such a thing would be typical for Florence, she enjoyed such outings. Brigges should know, after all he absorbed her and now knew everything about her.

Brigges knew Samuel Gates too. The love that he felt for Florence. The expectation of their forthcoming marriage. All of which he stole from them by murdering them and absorbing their forms so that he could pretend to be either of them. It suited his sick cravings when he was running rampant in London as Jack the Ripper. They both pointed at him and spoke as one, in perfect unison.

"You stole our futures from us. We could have been happily married but your insane lust for mayhem and murder robbed us of our lives! You deserve to be punished, and that is what is going to happen now!"

Even as the words finished Brigges flew into a panic. He was surrounded by ghosts of the people that he had killed so that he could take on their form. This wasn't supposed to happen. The dead are supposed to remain dead, harmless, gone. Instinct took over; he was so horrified of what was happening to him. He instinctively swam in the opposite direction only to be thwarted yet again.

Now it was Captain Benjamin Brigges himself, the *real* one. He floated there infuriatingly blocking the Siphonophore's escape route. He raised a finger pointing it directly between the eyes on the almost formless thing that the creature used as a head.

"You murdered my crew. You were responsible for the death of my wife and daughter! The time has come for you to face all of the evil that you have done!" Brigges face was contorting with fury.

The creature jerked from this way to that. There were more people in the water surrounding him now. Above and below, they were forming a net of floating human ghosts. He could see all of them. They were the people that he had murdered both directly and indirectly. All of his victims from his days being Jack the Ripper in London were there. All of the crew and passengers from the Mary Celeste. All of the miners from the Matlockite mine.

It was too much. The creature did not know that he could even feel as much dread and panic and terror that he did right now. It was consuming him. In horror he struck out at the closest ghost to him. He convinced himself in that microsecond that they were not real and could not possibly hurt him. He was wrong.

The tentacle struck one of the miners. The man grabbed it and crushed it with inhuman force between his fingers pulverising it. The searing pain raced through the Siphonophores body. He did not have a mouth but a high pitched shrill of agony was produced by something that approximated it.

They were solid. They were all around him he had no way to escape. The play of the heavy rain on the top of the river surface could be seen at a point though. It was a miracle. There was one place left that was not inhabited by these vengeful ghosts. It was directly up.

With every bit of force that he could muster, he pushed himself upwards and toward the surface of the river. They did not move to intercept him. Surely, they could see that he would be able to get away from them? But in his blind panic he did not consider or care. All he wanted to do was get away from the ghosts of his past murders.

The Siphonophore swam faster than he had ever done since becoming sentient and taking on his first human form. He burst through the surface of the river and hurled himself toward the muddy bank landing with a splash and thud.

He immediately took on his Benjamin Brigges form again so that he could better deal with being on land once more.

“There he is!” shouted someone from his side. Brigges spun around. It was Mary Whittaker. Now it was her that was pointing. Brigges could see that Keith Smedley, Thaddeus Tremorlund and William Aitkens were there. They were navigating the muddy river bank to apprehend him. For just one brief moment Brigges considered diving back into the water, but the thought of facing the dead people that were most certainly waiting there stopped him in his tracks.

He had to escape, on foot and on land. He attempted to get up and slipped over in the mud and crashed to the ground once more. He chanced a look to the approaching posse. They were gaining ground on him. Travelling more cautiously on the slippery riverbank. What horrors awaiting him from his own kind if they got close enough. He did not even want to contemplate it.

Clambering to his feet, he steadied himself and searched for the path that would get him away from his pursuers. He had to proceed agonisingly slowly for fear of losing his footing again. But it was working. He was able to get a few good footsteps in before almost falling again. Steadying himself with his hands, Brigges forced himself up the river bank and toward the roadway. If he could get to that he could make a dash for it.

The rain was not helping matters. It was heavy before and now looked to be getting nothing short of torrential. Bit by bit he made his way to the more sure-footed ground that led up to the road.

"If he gets up there he'll get away" shouted one of his pursuers to the others. But it was a moot point. He had managed to free himself of the muddy decline and was able to gain more traction here. He could feel the soft ground underfoot. It had more grass in it, which gave him the necessary adhesion. Soon he was up at the low stone fence that marked the side of the road facing the river. He grabbed it and jumped over like a show-dog. Landing with a splash on the wet road he righted himself to see how the people chasing him were doing.

They were closing. It only gave Brigges a moment to think of which direction to take in order to elude his executioners. The surrounding landscape was hard to see in the driving rain. It was hard to believe that it was still near to the middle of the day. The clouds were so dark as to almost blot out the sun.

The gorge that Matlock and Matlock Bath clung to rose up above him. Here it was less inhabited than Matlock. He would take his chances in the forested inclines above him. Surely, he would be able to elude them there.

Darting across the road he took the walking track stone stairs signposted saying that it would lead up to Waterloo Road and then on to Temple Road. There was a further sign pointing the way to the Temple Inn and Hotel. He wasn't that familiar with this section of the town. But upwards was his goal, he was determined to outrun and outsmart his hunters.

His arrogance was returning. He would be victorious. He had lived for years on his wits alone. This would be no different.

Encountering more of his own species was not what he expected. In fact, he had not even contemplated that there were any more like him in all of the years that he was stealing other people`s lives and making trouble. Now that he knew that there were more like him, it was not cathartic or liberating, it was the opposite. He detested them. They had been so arbitrary in passing judgement on him. How dare they. He would find a way to have his revenge on them no matter what it took or how long. Even as he climbed the stairs toward the Temple Inn he was using some part of his mind to plot the demise of both William Aitkens and Mary Whittaker. He would take pleasure in murdering Keith Smedley too. But last of all he would kill Thaddeus Tremorlund. Maybe in front of Tiffany? That thought pleased him.

Even better to murder the old woman first in front of the Mayor and tease him with it before relieving Thaddeus of his misery. The thoughts of murder and anarchy gave Brigges strength and he renewed his efforts to climb the stairs and make good his escape. He had a reason to live, so that he could continue to kill.

Chapter 29: The Temple Inn Hotel

William and Mary had been leading the pack, with Keith in the middle and poor old Thaddeus puffing behind them; quite some distance. Mary had spotted Brigges heading in the direction of the stairs. She knew Matlock Bath very well. This gave her the advantage in the pursuit of Brigges.

She indicated that William should follow her, and they bolted to the base of the stairs. Brigges could be seen at the very top of them before he disappeared from their view.

"After him!"she shouted.

They both bounded up the stairs with inhuman might. Keith had caught up by now and had to pause to catch his breath. He was bent over as he breathed deeply to regain his strength. He looked up at his cohorts. They did not appear to tire the way that a human being would. But maybe that shouldn't surprise him, he thought. Who knows what these human-replacing creatures were capable of. But, the enemy of my enemy is my friend; so, he would help them catch and stop this psychopathic murderer because it was the right thing to do. Renewed, he ran up the stairs after them.

By this time, Thaddeus had reached the bottom of the stairs. He looked up at the ascending Keith with a mixture of awe and horror. He couldn't believe the amount of physical exercise he had done in the last few minutes. It was certainly more than he had done in the entire previous month, he thought. He groaned loudly at the prospect of continuing, and up stars at that! But in Mayor Tremorlund's case it was self-interest and greed that was spurring him on. He would be let off the hook for the things that he had done, if he helped these creatures capture the wayward one of their kind. He would even be rewarded with the promised Chaumet Rings. They must be worth a small fortune by themselves. It was a win-win scenario. He couldn't have hoped for more.

All of a sudden, he felt that he could manage the stairs, so bracing himself, he began the long ascent to the top.

***

Thaddeus was the last to re-join the posse. They had assembled on Temple Road and were looking up and down. The rain had eased enough to give a better view of the surrounds, but not by much.

One building stood out amongst the smaller stone cottages. It was the Temple Inn and Hotel. It was taller, and the stone walls had been rendered and painted white.

"Let's see if he is hiding in there?" suggested William.

There were no opposing viewpoints or suggestions. And under the circumstances, it seemed the logical thing to do. Besides, it would be nice to get in out of the persisting driving rain. Even if it was for a short time.

They walked toward it. Arriving at the dark wood door, William opened it and allowed Mary, Keith and Thaddeus to enter before going in himself.

Inside it was warm and dry. The quaint beamed ceiling and panelled walls looked exactly as you would expect a nice establishment as this to look. The fireplace had a fire burning brightly.

"Come in, come in out of the rain. Warm yourselves by the fire."

The innkeeper looked like a jolly man. He was wearing a vest and the usual garb that was fashionable for innkeepers. His fulsome beard and moustache were joined with carefully waxed edges. It more than made up for the lack of hair on the top of his head.

"Mary Whittaker, lovely to see you gain. It's been too long since you've dropped by." He said recognising the local business owner immediately.

"Thank you Mister Jennings" she responded and made her way to the fire to warm up.

"Mayor Tremorlund; wonderful to have your patronage. May I get you all something?" he looked around at the group. There was a little bit of a puzzled expression on his face. He clearly couldn't ascertain why the four of them had been out in the rain. And probably wondering why none of them were at Easter Mass or Services. He looked more carefully at the remaining two men.

"Mister Aitkens of Rockside isn't it; and Mister Smedley of Smedley's surely?"

The innkeeper had correctly identified all four of the group. It did add to the vexed expression on his chubby features though.

"Just some information if you please Mister Jennings" said Mary.

"Has anyone else come by, have you seen anyone at all? We've lost one of our party and are searching for him. A man in his mid-thirties, dark hair and beard, answers to the name of Captain Benjamin Brigges."

Jennings scratched his beard and looked from Mary to the others.

"No, I haven't seen anyone. Were you going to meet him here?" he inquired

"We just thought that he may have taken shelter from the rain here. All of the other buildings nearby are residences. Yours is the only commercial establishment and we were hoping that he singled it out."

"Well don't be too concerned. Sit down and dry off and lct me get you all a nice Brandy to help you warm up. He may yet come along. You never know your luck?" Mister Jennings did not wait for a reply but made his way to the bar to make good on his tempting proposal.

Mary looked to William for guidance.

“We have to find Brigges. Maybe we should split up. Some go right the others left. Every moment we stay here, he could be getting further away.” She waited for his response.

William was more sanguine in the situation than she would have thought. He was regarding Mister Jennings with a frown on his face. He looked back at Mary and then spoke to the trio.

“Yes, I think that you are right Mary. We should split up. I’ll take Thaddeus and go down the road. You take Keith and go up the road. You know what to do if you find him.” William’s plan sounded immediate. The three moved to do as he said but he stopped them.

“But first let`s have a Brandy as Mister Jennings has suggested. It will bolster us before we continue our search.”

The news was unexpected but quite welcomed by Thaddeus and Keith. Both of whom gave a resolute ‘yes’ before taking a seat in two nearby armchairs. Each let out a resounding sigh as they sat.

Mary couldn’t believe what she was hearing. She was about to challenge him on the urgency of the situation they were in, but he cautioned her with a look. She did not quite understand it, but knew that he was up to something. Best to play along and see what it was.

Mister Jennings had prepared the drinks by then and was carrying a tray of four partially filled brandy glasses toward them. Mary and William found complimenting arm chairs near the fire, along side Keith and Thaddeus. The innkeeper handed them out one by one beginning with Mary, stating the recipients name in each case.

"There you go. Can I interest you in anything to eat? We have a cracking-good stew simmering in the kitchen. Warm your cockles that will?" he said winking as he finished his sales pitch. It sounded tempting, but they wouldn't be there long enough to be able to enjoy it. Once more William surprised them by saying something quite unexpected.

"Why don't you get Mary a small sample. If she likes it then we will all have a generous portion" he said offering a potential sale. This clearly pleased the innkeeper. He broke into a broad smile through his capacious beard and responded with glee.

"Right-oh. Off to the kitchen, I am. You won't be able to say no when you taste this Mary. I'll be as quick as I can!" he hurried to make good on his promise.

When he was gone Keith challenged him.

"Surely we have to keep up the pursuit of Brigges. He cannot be allowed to get away!"

William did not respond. He was looking intently into the glass of Brandy. He sniffed it and then tipped it towards his mouth and rudely poked out his tongue to let a bit of it touch its tip. He withdrew his tongue and closed his eyes as if savouring the drink.

His non-response was perturbing under the circumstances. Keith looked at Thaddeus who returned the look and simply shrugged. He was clearly on the side of drinking and eating before resuming the chase. Keith looked to Mary for support, but she was distracted by her own puzzled assessment of William's behaviour.

Thaddeus took in the aroma of the Brandy and swirled it in the bottom of the bulbous glass. Whatever Mister Jennings had served it certainly was a good one. He was lifting the glass to his lips when William jumped up from his seat and with one bound crossed to Thaddeus and knocked the glass violently from his hand.

The glass smashed against the fireplace and the brandy ignited causing a flash of burning alcohol. Thaddeus was incensed at the behaviour and of losing such a fine Brandy.

"It's poisoned!" he said

"What?" Thaddeus was horrified. He jumped up from his chair, as did Keith and Mary.

"A tasteless poison that we secrete from one of our glands. You wouldn't have known about it until it was too late. And it would have been an agonising death!"

William's explanation shocked them all.

"Jennings is Brigges" said Mary stating what had occurred to them all. It was obvious now. Brigges had taken shelter here from the rain after all and absorbed the only inhabitant. Everyone else was busy with Easter celebrations.

Keith tossed the brandy from his glass into the fire causing another flare-up. William and Mary followed suit. They rested their empty glasses on the mantlepiece.

"He must have known that our poison wouldn't affect us, surely?" asked Mary of William. She couldn't figure out why Brigges would bother. William dismissed the confusion.

"All he wanted to do was decrease the number of people pursuing him. It certainly would have done that!" he indicated to Keith and Thaddeus. They both guessed that the purported poison would have been instantly lethal. Each man shuddered at the thought.

The sound of a horse on the street outside alerted them to what was happening. Jennings was making good his escape. Either he had watched them secretly and seen that his plan to poison them all had failed; or he had not bothered and was absconding anyway. It did not matter. William wanted to check a fact that he was only partially aware of.

"There are stables out back?" he inquired of Mary.

"To the side" she said both correcting and confirming his assumption.

"Quickly!" shouted William pointing at the door. They all bolted to it flinging it open and racing through. Jennings had mounted a horse, bareback and was trotting back down Temple Road toward the high-street.

"After him" ordered William, but he was pointing toward the stables. Clearly, he wanted to even the odds and continue the pursuit on horseback. They all knew what to do. Racing toward the stables, they could see that there were three horses left. It was providence. One for each of them.

There was no time to saddle them up, so like Brigges, who had now taken the human-form of Jennings, they would simply have to ride without the normal horse livery. The doors to each of the stalls where reached by the trio and opened simultaneously. Keith was chivalrously going to help Mary up. He made to go to her aide, but she sprang onto the light brown coloured horse with blonde mane as if she was an American Indian. Thaddeus was looking around for something to assist him up. Keith elected to assist the Mayor instead.

William and Mary were once again ahead of them in the chase. With Thaddeus now ensconced on his mount Keith took his too. Both men nudged their horses into motion. The quest to stop Brigges was once more afoot.

Chapter 30: The Heights of Abraham

Chasing Jennings on horseback down steep roads that were perilously slippery from all the rain, was limited to a trot for the sections of Temple Road, Temple Walk and Waterloo Road. It wasn't until they descended to North Parade could the pace pick up somewhat. The driving rain had finally begun to ease and there was every sign that it may actually clear up.

The sight of the four bareback horse riders pursuing the Temple Hotel Innkeeper would have raised many an eyebrow if anyone had been around to see it. Jennings had not managed to get too much distance between himself and his hunters. Perhaps he was more of a poor horseman than the others. Whatever the reason, they were now in a better position to capture the errant Monster than they were when chasing him on foot.

Jennings glanced back and realised his precarious position. He angrily dug his heels into the flanks of the horse and shouted at it. The horse responded by picking up the pace. He knew this area of town well now that he had absorbed a local. So he aimed for the main bridge that crossed the river. He raced past the Jubilee Bridge that had been used earlier. The main bridge here in Matlock Bath was further up the main street.

Spurring-on his steed, he put a little more distance between himself and the posse in pursuit. Soon the bridge was in sight.

He was already coldly calculating an escape route. He briefly contemplated exiting the bridge to the water, but just as soon dismissed the idea. He did not relish the idea of landing in an underwater realm of ghosts again. No; this time he would have to make a proper escape over land.

He would deliberately tire the horses out by riding inexorably uphill. The others would eventually have to give up on compassionate grounds. But he did not care about the welfare of his mount. He would ride it until it died for all he cared. Jennings knew that it was his unfettered ruthlessness that would get him out of this situation.

He turned the corner and rode across the bridge, not even bothering to look down at the swollen river below.

***

Mary and William were in the lead, they were the next to cross the bridge. Keith and Thaddeus were following up from behind. From their point of view the next thing that happened was inexplicable. Both Mary and William pulled up their horses and craned their necks to the right as if trying to hear something. They looked at each other with a shared expression of surprise. But at what? When Keith and Thaddeus caught up to them, the two were consorting.

"Why have you stopped? What's wrong?" demanded Keith.

William and Mary looked at each other and somehow silently managed to agree that Mary should answer.

“It is another one of our kind. It has just arrived. It’s calling to us from beneath the river.” That was all of the explanation that she was prepared to give she dismounted and William steadied her mare whilst Mary walked to the edge of the bride and looked over. There was no sound, no sign that she was communicating with the newcomer; the sentient Siphonophore. But William assured the other two that that is exactly what was happening.

“Mary will fill-in the newcomer on what is happening and enlist its aide.”

Keith and Thaddeus could see that Mary was leaning over the bridge but could not make out any facial movement that may denote some form of communication. In answer to their unasked question William let them know that the way that Siphonophores communicate cannot be heard by human ears.

“It’s a series of pulses and silences of varying lengths, far too rapid for the human ear to perceive.” He hoped that it would quell their questions. He was correct. Both men looked like they were far more concerned with the escaping Jennings than the communications of a creature that before today they never even knew existed.

“Go on, we’ll catch up!” he instructed. Thaddeus and Keith needed no further prompting, they jostled their mounts into motion and were soon racing after the murderous creature once more.

Mary returned to her mount and updated William in Siphonophore language, saying that it had heard of the cluster of beings here in Matlock and wanted to become a part of the community. She told the newcomer of the errant Brigges and how he must be stopped. The newcomer agreed to take on a form and follow them as soon as it was able.

Keith was gratified to have the help. After Mary had once more safely taken her mount, they spurred their horses into motion and took of after Keith and Thaddeus.

***

The pursuit had gone exactly as Jennings had anticipated. He had taken every road that let to the heights of Abraham. So-named after the heights of Abraham in Quebec, Canada. The whole area was similar in topography to its Canadian namesake. It was high atop Masson Hill and the section that he had entered now was a zig-zagging path that was steep and led all the way to the top.

The rain had finally stopped, but the walking trail was muddy and slippery. That, combined with the excessive steepness of the tail, had once more brought the horseback pursuit down to an agonising crawl.

Jennings horse had a lather on it now. It was clearly distressed and tired, but he did not care. He cruelly jabbed the horse`s flanks with his heals. He would force it to take him to the very top. The horse objected by rearing-up a little and giving a loud neigh.

"Come on; come on!" he shouted in response to the animal`s protest. It was a well-trained horse and did as its rider instructed.

Further back Keith, Thaddeus, Mary and William had mercifully stopped their mounts. They could see Brigges high above them on the trail.

"He must be planning to ride that horse to death!" shouted Thaddeus.

"He is an absolute maniac!" quipped in Keith.

"I cannot push this poor beast any further William, we must rest them" Mary`s empathy for the plight of their horses was evident.

"You're right!" shouted William. He dismounted, and the others followed suit. Being stabled together they would naturally stay in a group together.

William set the scene for the rest of the pursuit up the walking trail.

"Thaddeus, you take the steed and walk it up the trail to the top, head for the Victoria Prospect Tower at the pinnacle of the hill. Mary and I can pursue Brigges faster in a hybrid form. Keith do your best to keep up."

The plan was simple but gave rise to multiple questions that both Thaddeus and Keith thought the better of, rather than asking. Both nodded their acquiescence.

William and Mary must have had some Siphonophore communication that Keith and Thaddeus could not be privy to, because they both started to glow green in the dull afternoon light. The bottom halves of their bodies began to lose shape. Just as quickly though, the parts of their hips downwards were reformed into something resembling a cross between a black bear and a gorilla.

Keith and Thaddeus's shock was short lived as both Mary and William bounded up the pathway at a speed that stunned both men. They looked at each other realising that it was now up to them to follow as best as they were able.

"See you at the top" said Keith in a brief but pertinent farewell to the Mayor. He took off after the bizarre pair.

"Indeed" said Thaddeus in an exasperated tone. He took the chin of the Steed that William had been riding and coaxed it to follow him up the pathway at a gentler speed. The horse complied, and the others followed willingly. He began a muddy ascent, squelching his way up the walking path.

***

Jennings looked down through the trees. He could see that William and Mary were in some weird sort of hybrid form and were chasing him up the hill with much more alacrity than his exhausted horse was able to provide. He growled with frustration.

“Two can play at that game” he said to them in his human voice. There was no hope of them hearing from this distance though. The walking trail was beginning to level off as he approached the summit of the hill. Ahead of him he could see the Victoria Prospect Tower that stood atop the hill.

Jennings dismounted his horse. He could walk the rest of the way. And then before his pursuers had any hope of catching him; he too would transform and flee them.

He was very unimpressed with the only two other sentient-Siphonophores that he had encountered. They were simply not pitiless enough to be any match for him. In fact, he loathed them. Perhaps instead of escaping he should lay a trap for them both, and their human consorts.

The idea appealed to him. But an old saying resonated in his mind. Discretion is the better part of valour. He would live to fight another day and plot their demise at some time in the future. Right now. all he needed to do was effectively escape their clutches.

Chapter 31: Victoria Prospect Tower

The Victoria Prospect Tower was built in 1844 to celebrate the reign of Queen Victoria. It was made of the local stone in a gothic-revival style. A typical castle-like turret with appropriate top. Stairs led to the pinnacle from which all of the surrounding hills and valleys could be seen in all of their splendour. There was an adjacent amphitheatre too. It was there that Jennings was heading. It would be easier to take a form and bolt down away from the other Siphonophores from there.

Something strange caught his eye. There was a young deer in the amphitheatre blinking at him. Perhaps wondering if the human was a threat. Jennings barely gave it a glance as he entered the stone semi-circular structure. He would need to pick out the most heavily forested side of the amphitheatre from which to make his escape. The trees would afford him the cover he would need. He looked around getting his bearings. The deer did not move. That was unusual. But Jennings didn't notice. He was too absorbed in the next phase of his escape plan.

He was walking along the highest part of the circle when he noticed some movement out of the corner of his eye. He spun around. The deer was there looking innocently at him.

Jennings briefly thought that it may be after food. Perhaps some bleeding-heart local had been feeding it and it had lost its fear of humans?

"Go!" he shouted at it, expecting it to take flight, it did not.

"Get out of here!" he shouted more loudly waving his arm threateningly. It did not react as expected. Rather than take flight, it actually moved closer. Looking both innocent and menacing at the same time. Something was wrong, Jennings knew that now. He regarded the animal more closely. The deer responded by taking another step closer to him. This time Jennings was the one that retreated. Somehow the tables had turned without him realising how, or why?

Jennings was about to make yet another attempt to scare the deer away when the animal started to glow a very familiar green. Immediately Jennings knew that he was facing another Siphonophore. He panicked.

He turned to run. There, he could see William and Mary now entering the clearing where the tower and amphitheatre were. One Siphonophore behind him, and two ahead, there was only one place to take refuge. The tower.

Jennings did something that he had never done before. He acted purely out of fright. There were three Siphonophores after him now. He had never before been in a position like this. These were his own kind. They would be more than capable of killing him. He was absolutely blinded with panic. He would have to have been, in order to think that the tower could offer him any refuge.

He darted for the entrance and ran through it mounting the stone stairs. Fear was enveloping him even has he thundered up the circular stairway. He barely glanced behind him at the entrance as he rounded the inside of the cylindrical tower, climbing upwards and upwards. He could see that William Aikens and Mary Whittaker and a new person had entered the tower, someone that he did not recognize. But for sure it was the Siphonophore that had previously masqueraded as a deer.

They were all after him. He actually let out a little yelp as he climbed without even realising that he had done it.

“There he is!” shouted William pointing at Jennings pounding his way up the stairs. Even at this distance the sound of Aitkens voice sent a shudder through Jennings. They all began their pursuit up the stairs after him.

Round and round the ever-climbing stairs they all ran. Jennings not even thinking for a moment what he would do upon reaching the turreted top of the tower. It was a reality that hit him fair in the face when he finally stumbled out onto the lookout area. The castellated walls affording a commanding view of the surrounding countryside. But that was all! There was no way to escape. He was trapped! Jennings spun around he could hear the footsteps of the others ascending the staircase. They would be with him in moments. He ran to the stone wall and looked directly down. There he could see Keith Smedley with Thaddeus Tremorlund someway behind approaching the tower and amphitheatre area. The Mayor still leading the horses, including the one that he had abandoned.

“There is nowhere to go Brigges….Jennings!” shouted Aitkens as he arrived on the lookout. Mary followed closely behind him and the other man. Jennings did not respond he was incapable of rational thought at this stage. He again looked down wondering if he could survive such a fall. There was no way that he could.

He turned around to face his captors. They had advanced upon him. A strange thing happened to Jennings. The face of each of the helpless victims that he had ever absorbed; murdered flashed before his eyes. It was as if the dead had come back to take vengeance upon him.

“Get away!” Jennings screamed. The note of horror evident in his voice.

“Don’t panic Jennings; it will be alright” Mary Whittaker’s words were so unexpected that Jennings froze. He looked at her. There was a glimmer of hope in his eyes. Perhaps they would not kill him after all? Maybe they were going to let him go?

But they were the thoughts of a desperate and deluded mind. Mary’s next words shattered his fanciful misconception.

“We will make your death quick and painless; just stand perfectly still!”

With is back to a surely fatal fall, and three Siphonophores surrounding him, Jennings had no chance. He growled at them and in a split second decided to rush them. He had one chance of getting past them. He would aim for the weakest point; Mary.

Just as he made that decision, Mary, William and the third Siphonophore opened their mouths and flicked out their tongues. They were impossibly long and slender and stretched beyond reason. Each became a tendril of uncanny speed. They all impacted Jennings at a different point of his body. One in the face, two on the torso. Something that looked like lightning shot through the tongue-tendrils and erupted inside Jennings. He shuddered. Time stood still.

Death was overcoming him. As it did a woman appeared before him. She was old but glowing with a white light that he had never seem the like of before. It was Alice Athalia. He looked at her with a vexed expression. How could she be here? Where had she come from? As if in answer to his questions, she spoke.

"And so, it ends. Your life of murder and mayhem, deceit and betrayal. It is a good thing that you will die, misshapen creature. There is nothing waiting for you here in the afterlife. For you see, hell is not a place of eternal damnation. What have you ever done to deserve immortality? Hell is not being able to be reborn as a higher form of life. You and everything that you have ever been will be snuffed out like a candle in a breeze. You have amounted to absolutely nothing."

She smiled at him. It seemed like a kind smile, but it cut through Jennings harder than the sharpest knife. And for a second time in the same day, he felt something that he had never felt before; but this time it was regret.

“no!” he said feebly as Alice Athalia disappeared before his eyes and he and fell forward. His body hit the flagstones. Mary, William and the stranger looking over him.

“It’s done” said William stating the very obvious. They stood there for a long time looking down at the lifeless body of Mister Jennings. Eventually Keith Smedley and even Mayor Tremorlund joined them at the top of the lookout.

Thaddeus was huffing and puffing as he arrived, quite some time after Keith.

“You got him; good show” he said trying to catch his breath.

Keith and Thaddeus now had the time to look at the stranger. He was not someone that they had seen before.

Mary and William and he appeared to be in some form of non-verbal communication. They looked at each other and there were facial expressions and nodding and shaking of heads. Something was being decided. But it was not the privy of the two humans present.

The stranger leant over and touched the body of Jennings with both hands. He began to glow green. Before the amazed eyes of Keith and Thaddeus the stranger took on the form of Mister Jennings the innkeeper. Both men blinked and looked at him and then down at the lifeless form of Mister Jennings lying at their feet. It was a surreal experience.

There was more ‘talking’ between the sentient-Siphonophores. They leant forward together to touch the body of Jennings. Something happened immediately to it. It began to deflate, as if someone had let out all of the air. Then it began to liquify and lose its shape. Clothes, features, limbs all were unrecognisable now. The mass of ooze began to thin and trickle under their shoes. Keith and Thaddeus jumped out of the way not wanting any of the liquid to touch their boots. There were however three rings that had surfaced from the diminishing liquid. These must have been the three Chaumet rings that had been promised to Thaddeus in payment for continuing to assist the creature.

Before long there was nothing left of the murderous creature. The Monster of Matlock was dead; dead and decomposed. There was nothing left of it but a slimy colourless sludge on the flagstones of the Victoria Tower lookout. Thaddeus made to bend down and recover the rings, but Mary beat him to it. He gave her a look of annoyance. He was about to admonish her when William spoke.

“Lots to do gentlemen” said William addressing the Mayor and Keith Smedley. This took them both aback somewhat.

“The creature is dead, there is no evidence that it ever existed; what has had to be done, has been done.” The Mayor’s pragmatic appraisal of the situation could not be argued with.

Mary spat out a sentinel-urchin at Thaddeus it caught him in the neck. He reacted as you would expect.

“What on earth!” he said in an irritated tone and then completely forgot what he was objecting about.

Keith was horrified. He turned to William just in time to see him spit an urchin his way. It hit Keith in the neck too. He was about to object when all of a sudden, he couldn't remember what he was about to say. William addressed Keith.

"You will forget the Mayor's confession about his murder of Martha Morrell. You will forget all about the Monster of Matlock. It has been an aberration only. Nothing of substance has ever been proven. The unfortunate and inexplicable murder of Martha Morrell may never be solved. You will forget everything that you have witnessed about our kind, the Siphonophores here in the village. Do you understand?"

Keith was already forgetting the things that he had been told to forget. It was so easy to do so. It was exactly what he wanted to do more than anything. A peace began to fill him. He had been so anxious over the last couple of months. But it was all for nothing. He had nothing to worry about, everything was fine.

He smiled and nodded slowly to William. Mary addressed the Mayor.

"You will forget everything to do with murdering the miners, and Martha Morrell and encountering the Siphonophores here in the village. I will return with you to your home and await your lovely wife. I have some words for her as well. Yes?" she looked at Thaddeus for a signal of affirmation. He smiled and nodded. He couldn't quite remember what he had been told to forget but he was glad to oblige.

Jennings walked over and peered over the edge of the lookout.

"All of the horses are below. I'll take them back to the inn. If anyone asks, I decided to take them for a walk as the rain had stopped."

"Perfect" said Mary.

"I think that should take care of all the loose ends. We won't need to explain the disappearance of Mister Jennings. The only three humans that know of our kind have had or will soon have those pertinent memories erased. Life in Matlock can go back to normal."

William looked to his two cohorts for confirmation that he had covered everything. They nodded in acquiescence.

Epilogue:

Life returned to normal very quickly for Matlock. The murder of Martha Morrell was fodder for much speculation for many years to come. There was even an outrageous notion that Jack the Ripper had returned from obscurity to perpetrate the heinous act. But no substantial evidence was ever found that pointed with certainty to a killer.

Matlock had had a run of bad luck with a couple of hapless people falling from the cliff walking track. There was that horrible accident with dynamite in the Matlockite mine that killed seven miners. But as quickly as the awful sequence of events had started it was all over.

The town continued to prosper with the growing popularity of the mineral hydro establishments. The new one opened by Job Smith was the crown of the town. Along with the cable-car tram to take people up the unforgiving hill, it made Matlock the town to beat when it came to taking-in the healing waters.

The Siphonophores lived amongst the townsfolk in complete secrecy. Within their own ranks they remembered the time that a psychotic one of their number almost ruined it for them all. But disaster had been averted and life was back to the way that it should be.

The End

Connect with Aenghus Chisholme

Visit my website on www.aenghuschisholme.com

Other Books by Aenghus Chisholme

Merlin the Sorcerer AD491

King Arthur is facing a war with the murderous Saxon Lord Aelle over the artisan land of Anderidae. Unknown to him magical forces have conspired with Aelle to ensure Arthur's defeat.

Guinevere the Queen AD494

Queen Gwenhwyvar and Sorceress Morgan Le Fay pursue the stolen Excalibur to a magical labyrinth where it is guarded by powerful Minotaur.

Sir Guaen and the Green Knight AD499

An animated corpse has Sir Guaen in its sights. How can you kill something that is already dead?

Arthur the King AD517

Caught in an untenable situation King Arthur is manoeuvred into a battle he cannot possibly win.

Murder on the Mary Celeste

One by one the passengers and crew aboard the Mary Celeste are being murdered. Alone and far from help they grapple with the reality that it is one of their number committing these hideous crimes.

Jack the Ripper: The Murder of Madam Athalia

London 1888: The Ripper is murdering with impunity. When an old Psychic is killed in her stately manor home away from the slums of the inner city only one clever young Detective sees a similarity. If he can figure it out, he may just be the one that can capture Jack the Ripper.

The Best Things in Life Begin with the Letter B

Curate your twenty-first century life with expert guide Aenghus Chisholme as he parades before you the exclusive and the everyday to bring into focus that regardless of cost, the best things in life really do begin with the letter B.

Commissioned Works

Got something on your mind and would like me to write it for you? Let me know what it is that you want. We'll work out a way to get it done.

www.ingramcontent.com/pod-product-compliance
Lightning Source LLC
LaVergne TN
LVHW091027080826
845145LV00002B/387